RUGGED EDGES

NANCY PIRRI

ISBN: 978-1-68046-967-7

Published by Satin Romance
An Imprint of Melange Books, LLC
White Bear Lake, MN 55110
www.satinromance.com

Published in the United States of America.

Cover Design by Caroline Andrus

This one's for you, Laura, because of Wiley.

CHAPTER ONE

June
Present Day San Antonio Texas

Gina Liberatti didn't reach for the phone when it rang. She had a secretary to take her calls. Her attention was completely focused on the amazing 'before' and 'after' shots of her latest client. The physical changes in Mrs. Amelia Murphy were profound, even though the items Gina had suggested the woman alter were minimal.

The shorter hairstyle removed ten years from the woman's appearance. Taupe-colored eye shadow and peach blush were more natural appearing than Mrs. Murphy's previous signature make-up of harsh blue shadow and stop-sign-red lipstick. But Gina's recommendation of a minor facelift made an astonishing difference.

That's what people paid Gina to do; to polish their appearance. Gina's relatively newfound vocation in life as an image consultant was fulfilling, albeit not as prosperous as she would have liked, but the business was steadily growing.

Money had never meant a whole lot to her while her husband had lived, but it did now. Since Charlie died, she learned raising two sons on one income wasn't easy. But she sure was thankful Charlie'd had an insurance policy through the company he worked, which paid her well upon his death, hence how she managed to start her consulting business in the first place.

Because she had two children, she chose to grow slowly, working only four days a week, no more than five hours a day. She loved her less than full time work schedule, and the flexibility.

The phone's persistent ringing gained her attention. Looking down at the phone's panel she saw it was her secretary buzzing her. She punched the speaker button. "I'm here, Ruby."

"Your four o'clock appointment arrived five minutes ago."

Gina frowned as she sank against the back of her ergonomically correct chair and proceeded to absently tap the end of the pen against her desk blotter. "I thought Miss Schneider canceled for today."

"She did, but I filled the spot. Remember?"

Gina didn't recall but wasn't surprised. She had a lot on her mind lately; in particular, her fifteen-year-old son's latest attempts at becoming a first-class juvenile delinquent. Gina had spent a small fortune on psychologists, but Jack had charmed them all. Heavens, they made it sound like *she* was the problem, not her kid! And forget the school counselors; they were so busy dealing with the really hard cases her son appeared angelic in comparison.

"You know, Gina, the more I look at this guy, the more I think we should send him on his way," Ruby murmured.

"What's wrong with him?"

"He'll be quite a challenge."

"That's what people pay us to do for them, Ruby, make changes —some more than others."

"Well, you might want to rethink this one because he's sort of, well…hairy."

"What?" Gina wondered if she'd heard right.

2

"I'll just show him in."

"Good idea. Give me a sec, though."

Gina knew by her secretary's cryptic reply that this potential client wasn't husband material. Ruby was always on the lookout for a husband—number three this time—which Gina couldn't understand at all. One husband had been enough for her. Just before she depressed the speaker button, she heard Ruby say softly, "My, oh, my."

"Ruby? Are you still there?"

"He's in front of the magazine rack," Ruby said, her voice a muffled whisper. "Now he's bending over, waaaay over, and—Sweet Jesus," she softly growled.

Gina kept her voice calm though she felt like shrieking at the top of her lungs. "What in the world is going on out there?"

When her secretary didn't reply Gina slammed down the phone, scrambled from her seat and crossed the office. With a hand on the doorknob she bent to retrieve one of the beige high-heeled shoes she'd kicked off earlier, which had landed behind the door.

As she slid her foot inside the shoe the door suddenly opened and smacked her hip.

"Ahhh!" she screamed as she toppled to the floor, landing on her hands and knees. She looked up and scowled into Ruby's surprised expression until she noticed the tall, brawny, red-eyed beast towering behind her.

Okay, so his irises were brown, but the whites of his eyes were definitely bloodshot. She could only assume he hadn't slept much last night or had been on a hell of a bender. She stared at him until she had a vague idea of what the man, not a beast after all, looked like beneath long sideburns, bushy mustache, and full, thick dark beard. She couldn't help but wonder what he was hiding behind all that hair.

He looked fierce and intimidating until she met his warm, sherry-colored eyes, the corners crinkling with humor. Somehow his dark-brown, wavy hair touching the wrinkled collar of his shirt made him appear a bit more approachable than she'd initially thought.

"Well, I'll be damned," he said in a strong, Texan drawl.

Ditto. Gina was already fairly certain she'd be damned if she took him on as a client. Yet, with his dust-covered, hopelessly rumpled clothing, scuffed boots and all that hair he'd be her most challenging client to date. Luckily, these were all external improvements that should be easy to change. Now a man's character was an entirely different matter.

Gina hadn't noticed his battered black Stetson until he handed it to Ruby then edged around her, moving forward into Gina's office.

Ruby held the hat at arm's length, away from her sleek red dress. It took all of Gina's fortitude to keep a straight face.

He bent slightly, then lowered his hands toward Gina. "Allow me."

She liked the fact he waited for her nod before he took her hands and pulled her to her feet.

She didn't mean to be impolite, but she couldn't help but sweep a lingering look over his body. He was at least six-four and built like a linebacker. He also appeared right at home in a pair of too snug, faded jeans that encased his long legs.

Gina was not a woman who ignored a good-looking guy in a pair of tight jeans but his were also an inch too short, possibly relics from his younger years while he was still growing. His wide shoulders stretched the fabric of his chambray shirt, the cuffs rolled back to reveal strong, hairy forearms.

Her cheeks turned hot when she saw the appreciative look in his eyes. "Thank you," she murmured as she tugged on the hem of her fawn-colored jacket and smoothed down the matching pencil skirt.

"Sorry, boss," Ruby apologized. "What were you doing behind the door?"

"Retrieving my shoes," she said, thinking that's what she got for kicking them off, as she did between appointments.

Starting to reach for the shoe, Gina paused when the man offered, "I'll get it." He went down on one knee, scooped the shoe up in his big hand and grinned up at her. "Better hold on to my shoulder, darlin'."

Hold on? Darling?

He took her foot and raised it off the floor. She wobbled on the other foot with a gasp then latched onto one of his broad shoulders. It was either that or fall on her butt. The warm sensation of his hand on her calf as he slid on her shoe prompted her to think silly thoughts of Cinderella. As she stared down at his shaggy head, she decided he didn't look like the prince in that particular fairy tale, but resembled the huge, furry beast from another.

"Thanks." She felt heat seeping into her cheeks.

His gaze was still focused on her shoes as he rose to his full height. "They're pretty." He folded his arms across his chest and added, "Though I thought ladies nowadays liked comfortable, athletic-style shoes."

"If one is in to exercising, perhaps."

Gina's idea of exercising didn't include working up a sweat. Playing a tame game of pool or table tennis with her sons was more her speed. Belatedly, she noted that her hand was still on his shoulder so she withdrew it.

He sent her another one of his captivating grins, even white teeth flashing in deep contrast against his tanned complexion. Gina couldn't help but return his smile. Then she waved her hand toward a chair positioned in front of her desk.

"Please, have a seat."

In two strides he stopped beside the chair, an expectant look on his face.

She strode behind her desk, sat down in her seat, and decided she couldn't quibble about his manners. Stretching out her hand, she said, "I'm happy to meet you, Mister—?"

"Mitchell. Stone Mitchell." He reached out and grasped her hand.

Gina smiled. "Tell me about yourself, Mr. Mitchell."

"I own Falcon's Ridge Ranch, about two hours southwest of here," he announced with undisguised pride. "You come highly recommended, Miz Liberatti."

"Why, thank you."

"Excuse me, Gina?"

She looked up and met Ruby's eyes as she stood in the doorway. "Yes?"

"Do you need anything before I leave for the night?"

Gina glanced at her watch "It's only four-fifteen. You're leaving already?"

"I have a doctor's appointment. Remember?"

"Oh! I'd forgotten." Maybe *she'd* better make a doctor's appointment, a tiny voice inside chastised her. There wasn't a thing wrong with her memory, but then again, her eldest son's recent escapades drove her to distraction.

"Would you please bring us some coffee before you leave?"

"Sure thing." Ruby moved to Stone and handed him back his hat. "I'll be back in a jiffy."

Gina turned her attention back to Stone.

He tossed his hat on the chair beside him as he looked around. "Nice place."

"Thank you." She smiled her appreciation.

She'd decorated the office in tones of mauve and navy. A Berber carpet of burgundy with flecks of blue covered the floor. A navy blue leather sofa and matching chairs were grouped for easy conversation. It was a classic, yet comfortable look.

Ruby returned with a large tray where she balanced a thermal coffee server alongside a creamer and sugar bowl, and two white coffee mugs. She set the tray down on the desk, leaned forward and poured two cups of coffee. "Cream or sugar?"

"Black, please."

She slid the cup across the desk toward him then settled back in her chair. She glanced up in time to see Ruby back out of the office, a scowl on her pretty face.

"I'll see you in the morning, Ruby. Have a good night."

Gina ignored her secretary's wide-eyed, apprehensive look and smiled at the big man sitting comfortably across from her.

"Now then, what can I do for you, Mister Mitchell?"

She heard the door close, satisfied Ruby had left for the night. She didn't feel a need to heed her secretary's warning look. For some incomprehensible reason she felt perfectly safe with this stranger.

"I'd like to hire you, Miz Liberatti. A neighbor of mine, Stan Jenkins, said you did wonders for him." He frowned and crossed one snakeskin booted ankle over his knee. "Hmm, the more I think about it, it might have been his wife who said it, not him."

Vivid memories of the hard-core cowboy-rancher for whom she'd performed somewhat of a miracle on months ago came to mind. Stan Jenkins was from the old school of thought on bathing —every Saturday, and only on Saturday. The man was a rancher who worked hard and copiously sweated because of it. She'd managed to convince him his new wife wasn't out of line expecting him to shower every day. The whisker and hair trim and a few sets of new clothing hadn't hurt either.

She leaned forward, her hands around her cup. "Do you understand my line of work?"

"Stan explained everything to me."

Gina saw a tinge of pink appear on his neck above his shirt collar, just below his beard. "What did Mister Jenkins tell you?"

"He said you made a gentleman out of him."

"Stan Jenkins was a perfect gentleman from the moment we met. I simply advised him in selecting new clothes, instructed him on proper table manners, and encouraged him to get a decent haircut and to shower more often."

"Sounds good to me."

Gina raised her brow. "Are you telling me you'd like the same advice?"

Stone set his own cup down on the desk. He reached up and raked his overly long hair off his forehead. But as soon as he removed his hand it fell forward again. "I haven't had a haircut in a while."

Or a shave, she noted.

"Haven't had much time since I've been mending fences and moving cows for the past month, pretty much non-stop." He paused then a discomfiting look on his face. "There's something else I'd like you to do; teach me how to dance."

"Excuse me?"

"I'm an awful dancer," he admitted. "Maybe you could help me choose some new clothes, too."

She gave him the once over again and decided his was a very tempting proposition. "My rates are one-hundred and twenty-five dollars an hour, and I require a two-hundred-dollar retainer when you sign a contract, non-refundable."

"That's all?" he asked.

She gave him a cool smile. "They're competitive for the area, Mister Mitchell. Sure, we can do some dance lessons. By the time I'm through with you, folks will be calling you Fred Astaire."

He cracked his knuckles and nodded. "Hot damn—uh—that's great."

"May I ask why you feel compelled to make these changes?"

"I've decided it's past time I married," he announced.

Gina leaned forward with a broad smile. "So, who's the lucky lady?"

"That's the problem. I haven't done any serious courting, but my goal is to be married by Christmas."

Good grief! Christmas is only six months away. Gina sank back in her chair with a sigh.

"So, you're telling me you don't have a fiancée?"

He shook his head, staring down at his boots.

"How about a girlfriend?" she asked gently, guessing his answer, and yet hoping she was wrong.

"Like I said, I haven't devoted a lot of time to wife hunting. Now that the ranch is up and running smoothly, though, I'm ready to tackle the job."

He made looking for a wife sound like any other ranch chore, and Gina found it hard to believe women weren't calling him all hours of the day and night. In a rough, rugged way, he was handsome, and he did have his own spread.

"I've someone in mind, though," he offered.

Gina sighed in relief. "Wonderful. Tell me about her."

"She's a widow lady who owns the ranch next to mine, The Rockin' J. She has hundreds of acres of grazing land, and deep wells that won't run dry any time soon."

Criminey! I asked about the woman and he's raving about land and wells.

"About those dance lessons, Miz Liberatti..." He tugged uncomfortably at his collar. "I have to tell you I've two left feet when it comes to waltzin' a lady around the dance floor." He shrugged and muttered, "Never been any good at it."

"You know, many women could care less about dancing," she said gently.

His face colored again. "Maybe, but Rachel goes line-dancing every Saturday night. So you'd need to teach me how to do that too. I figure it can't hurt to learn."

Gina eyed his long hair and beard. "I'm sure once we make some changes in your appearance your neighbor will be very interested in you, if she isn't already."

"Maybe." He rubbed his lips with a thumb, a thoughtful look on his face. "I guess it wouldn't hurt for me to learn to talk a bit more refined, too."

His low, soft drawl was pleasant, but she hadn't missed the sprinkling of light profanities in his speech.

"Right. Is there some pressing reason why you must marry by Christmas?"

Gina's heart plummeted when she saw the uncomfortable expression on his face. She cursed herself for asking his reasons for marrying so soon and listened intently to his reply.

"I've spent many a Christmas alone since I haven't any family. I'll be thirty-five next month and it's time I settled down. Christmas is a joy-filled time of year. It just seems like the right time."

"I understand." And she did. Who was she to judge him when she'd only known her husband six months before marrying him?

"So, teach me how to dance, give me advice on buying new clothes and remind me not to cuss, then I'll be ready to go courting."

"Don't forget the haircut." She tilted her head to one side and stared at him. "You know, you may want to shave off the beard and mustache as well."

His dark expression told her he had no intentions of budging on the issue, including responding to her suggestion.

Gina decided she'd take up that particular crusade later. She came to her feet and extended her hand. "I do believe we've a deal. I'll draw up a contract first thing in the morning."

As Stone rose, he reached out and clasped her hand. "I'm looking forward to working with you." He released her hand and stretched his arms wide. "How about a dance lesson right now? There's no time like the present, I always say."

Gina stared at his massive body and eager expression and sighed. He was something else. She leaned down, opened a drawer, and pulled out her monthly planner. Call her old-fashioned but while she also used her email-outlook calendar, and she used the cloud for storage, she'd had her share of technology issues in the past and still depended on a paper trail back-up for her appointments.

"Today is Wednesday. It appears I should be finished with two of my clients by Friday, which will free up my time considerably." She met his eyes. "I really can't fit you in before Monday."

"How about Saturday?"

"My weekends are reserved for my children."

He frowned. "We've got a problem then, I'm afraid. As I mentioned earlier, my ranch is two and a half hours away, which makes it damn—er—darned hard for me to get away during the week. I'll meet you here at five on Saturday."

She narrowed her eyes at him, thinking he'd perfected the art of persuasion. He reminded her of a steamroller rolling over everything in his path in order to have things his way. She'd love to argue, doubting folks rarely challenged him, but decided not to push her luck. He'd learn soon enough she controlled her own life aside from the fact she needed the pay.

She couldn't allow him to slip through her fingers, for it seemed with every satisfied customer, she earned another by word of mouth. Her goal was to build up her clientele if she had any hope of tucking a substantial amount of money into her boys' college funds. She thought about her household chores, grocery shopping and chauffeuring the boys to and from baseball practice on Saturday and figured she'd be free by three.

"Saturday around five is fine."

"What about your kids?"

"Things wind down by mid-afternoon."

"Then your husband takes care of them?"

She wondered about his innocent expression. Was it possible he was fishing to see if she was married? No, he hadn't shown the least interest in her as a woman. Well, perhaps that wasn't true. She'd seen the way he'd looked her over when he'd assisted her with her shoe. But then she thought about the neighbor rancher-woman he planned on courting and decided his once over earlier was innocent.

"I'm a widow."

His cheeks colored. "Uh, sorry. Why don't you add the cost of a baby-sitter in your fee?"

She laughed. "My sons would take great offense at your name-calling. They're twelve and fifteen. I've an elderly neighbor who keeps an eye on them for no charge."

"Good." He gave her a contemplative look. "Before I leave, just off the top of your head, do you see anything I could work on between now and Saturday?"

He was tall and powerfully built. Unfortunately, his clothes appeared as clean as they could get due to their hard use and age. One shirttail hung over his belt while the other had been haphazardly tucked into his waistband.

She twirled her finger in a circle, indicating he should turn around. He complied and she moved up behind him. Reaching high she lightly smoothed the chambray fabric along his broad shoulders, down the length of his arms to his wrists, noting the snug fit.

Her hands tingled.

She moved around to his front, gazed at his tanned neck and broad chest.

Her heart raced.

Then she made the mistake of meeting his eyes. Her breathing quickened when she noted his appreciative look. This wasn't the first time she'd been this close to a male client before, but never had she experienced this heart-pounding sensation. This rugged cowboy was turning her on! So much for thinking his look earlier had been an innocent one. This guy was lethal to women, even with all of his whiskers.

The telephone rang, startling them both. Gina backed away from him, toward the phone. "Excuse me." She snatched it up on the second ring, then turned her back on him facing the windows.

———

Stone hadn't missed the relieved look in her eyes when the phone rang. He disturbed her, which was fine with him since she disturbed the hell out of him.

She was a lovely sight with her short, turned up nose, defiant chin, and wide eyes the color of light chocolate. The long length of her tawny hair reminded him of a lion's mane, and she smelled like raspberries. At first, he hadn't been certain from where the scent generated, until he caught a whiff of her hair. She must have washed it with raspberry-scented shampoo.

He swept her a long look from head to toe, lingering on her curvy ass, one of the finest he'd seen in all of San Antonio—maybe in all of Texas. After a while, he moved closer, focusing on her voice, tried making out her words. Though he'd left his life behind as a Texas Ranger, it didn't stop his cop's intuition from kicking in. After eavesdropping a moment he realized she was more than a bit irritated with the person on the other end.

Abruptly, she ended the conversation and slammed down the phone. She turned to him, her lips thinned, but she quickly lifted them into a false smile. "Sorry about the interruption. It was—" She leaned back against her desk, stopping herself.

He folded his arms and quirked one eyebrow. "Everything all right?"

"Oh, yes, just peachy keen."

"You're sure?" He frowned when she wouldn't meet his eyes.

"Absolutely."

He nodded and said, "You were about to give me some advice before the phone rang."

She looked up and he saw the confusion in her eyes until she suddenly remembered. "Yes, that's right."

He felt hot under the collar and stroked his beard self-consciously when she deliberately moved her gaze over every inch of him. Damn! Never would he do that to a woman again, he mused, chagrinned. It was embarrassing.

After a long silence, he growled, "Well?"

"I suggest you go up one size in your clothing."

He slammed a hand against his chest as though she'd stuck a knife in him. "Hell. Are you talking about my shirt size?"

"Pants, too. And I didn't know hi-rise jeans were in style any longer."

Stone caught the twinkle in her eyes and grimaced down at his worn jeans. "I've had these for a while…" Okay, so he'd had the jeans since right after college. Hell, they'd fit fine until then, but he'd grown another inch and half after college, which surprised the hell out of him. He was now six foot three and half inches tall and had put on extra pounds too. But he worked hard on his ranch so didn't carry an ounce of fat. "Just when I got 'em broke in the way I like 'em," he muttered.

"Walk away from me, please, toward the door," she ordered.

With a big grin on his face he strode across the room, swiveled on his boot heel, and came back, stopping directly in front of her.

"Shorten your stride a bit," she suggested, "and don't swing your shoulders so much from side to side."

His grin slipped but he walked back and forth again, stopping in mid stride when she laughed.

"Sorry," she murmured. "Your legs are stiff as a board. There's no need to be self-conscious. With the exception of a bit of a swagger, your walk needs little improvement."

His scowl deepened. "Then why in the hell—why did you tell me to change it?"

She shrugged. "You seem compelled to have me find something to correct."

"I don't swagger."

"Sure you do." She tilted her head to the side and examining him more. "Although I must admit it does seem to work for you."

Stone couldn't recall when a woman made him feel more self-conscious. Did he really want to subject himself to her scrutiny and her ideas of change? He was ready to call off the deal when he remembered the favorable improvements she'd made in his neighbor.

He'd set himself a goal to marry soon. He'd endure the woman's blasted changes, but once he married, he'd return to wearing his comfortable, worn clothing, and grow his hair to his shoulders if he wanted to. But no way was he shaving off his sideburns and beard. They had their purpose, concealing the wicked knife scar running down the left side of his face, from temple to chin, along his hairline.

His career as a Texas Ranger had been relatively short-lived, yet they'd felt like the longest years of his life. His biggest worry was that no woman would ever want to marry him if she saw the scars he'd sustained, both physically and mentally.

Which was the reason he'd come to Gina for help. He needed to improve his chances if he expected to convince his neighbor, Rachel Williams, to marry him. She had plenty of guys calling on her— some of them strong competition.

Settling his Stetson squarely on his head, he tipped the brim down just the way he liked. "See you Saturday. By the way, when do you think we can fit in that shopping trip?"

"Ah, yes," she murmured then returned to her desk and reached inside the drawer for her calendar again. "How about next Wednesday evening? Stores here in San Antonio are open until ten. You could meet me here when I'm done with work around five. I'm sure my neighbor would stay with the boys longer."

"Sounds good to me." He tipped his hat and headed for the door. With his hand on the knob he glanced at her over his shoulder. "See you Saturday."

After he left, Gina moved to the windows overlooking Flores Street. There was something about his smooth, low-timbered voice that made her want him to keep talking. She stared at the traffic below until her new client appeared. He swaggered across the street and every female he passed halted to stare at him. It was hard to tell from this distance if their expressions held admiration or terror.

She'd need to stay alert around this cowboy because his confident, albeit somewhat arrogant manner was too appealing. After growing up with her dominating father then marrying Charlie, she'd long ago made the decision to be her own woman and not live under the thumb of any man again. Decisions regarding her life and boys would be hers to make, whether right or wrong.

She thought about the disturbing phone call from her eldest son and started chewing on one fingernail. Jack had been suspended from school for smoking on school property. This was the second time in as many weeks. She'd reached her rope's end and hadn't figured out a way to make him obey. Denying him privileges hadn't worked; grounding him hadn't done any good, either.

The death of his father a year ago had hit him hard. At first, she'd been sympathetic toward him and had taken his rebellious behavior in stride, but not anymore. If he didn't want to find himself living in a court-ordered foster home he'd learn to follow hers and his school's rules. She'd heard about 'tough-love'. One of the families in her neighborhood had attended some of the tough love meetings held at a nearby Lutheran church. She made a mental note to call that neighbor tomorrow. It was way past time she got tough with Jack.

CHAPTER TWO

S aturday morning started out on a wrong note when Gina's washing machine broke down. She'd shoved the first load in at seven in the morning. Twenty minutes later she found herself slipping and sliding through an inch of soapy water across her laundry room floor.

Finding a repairman was impossible on a Saturday so she scheduled an appointment with a repair company for Monday afternoon. Then she loaded her laundry into the car, dropped her boys off at baseball practice and made her way to the nearest Laundromat. She spent the rest of the morning and early afternoon there, until it was time to pick up the boys, arriving home with just enough time to get ready to meet her newest client.

She'd also made a call to her neighbor and learned about the tough love meetings at Christ Emmanuel Church every Thursday evening. No one had answered the phone at the church, but she'd left a message asking if she could attend the next meeting. She needed help handling Jack. All of her understanding and leniency because of his father's death hadn't helped him one bit.

Now, standing before her closet mirror, she struggled with the zipper on a black sleeveless dress, giving up when she realized she'd need to call one of her sons to help. She slipped her feet into a pair of high-heeled sandals, cringing when she heard Jack, in the living room, spewing four-letter words.

As she hurried down the hallway, she decided Jack could teach Stone Mitchell a thing or two about cursing. She halted in front of the TV, jammed her hands on her hips and glared between her boys who sat on either end of the sofa.

"Tell me I didn't just hear the Lord's name taken in vain."

Jack peered up at her with a guilty expression. "It might a slipped out, but Chris took away the remote when it's my turn to use it."

"No more cursing, Jack, understand?"

Jack thinned his lips and nodded curtly.

Gina turned to her younger son. "Chris, give your brother the remote."

He clutched it. "But, Ma, I know after you leave, he won't give it back when it's my turn."

"Yes, he will." Her eyes returned to Jack. "Won't you?" At Jack's complacent shrug Chris scowled but tossed the controller to him.

Gina nodded. "Now behave yourselves. Mrs. Murphy is home and available for you to call if there are any problems. Okay?"

Jack and Chris groaned.

Gina guessed they'd put up an argument about their elderly, slightly eccentric neighbor checking in on them, as she did the few days a week when Gina worked. As it is, the woman kept a loose eye on them all summer long, too, but Gina didn't feel they were old enough to stay all day alone without any accountability to someone before a fight would ensue. With her neighbor available and checking in on them, they wouldn't dare fight. For brothers that were only three years apart, she wished they were closer, but it seemed the older they got the worse the fights, and more fighting and over stupid, silly things. Yet, for all of the arguments, the boys were close and got over their arguments quickly.

She sighed and looked down at her watch. Between travel time and Stone's appointment, she'd calculated she'd be away from the house at least three hours.

"If you don't want to check in with her while I'm gone come to the office with me."

Jack exploded, "No way!"

She smiled, knowing with that warning she'd have their full cooperation. She'd brought them to work with her on occasion, and they'd complained each time. With supremely male audacity, Jack had said her work stunk, but never again repeated the words once Gina reminded him that her stinking work provided them their bread and butter, not to mention a second-hand ping-pong table and a brand new Sony PlayStation with several games of their choosing.

"We won't fight," Jack promised. "At least not until you get back."

Gina rolled her eyes. "Thanks a heap." She turned around, headed for the dining room, and grabbed her purse from the table. "Now remember, showers by seven-thirty. I'll likely be back right around that time, if not before." She quickly made her way to the front door and opened it but stopped when Jack cleared his throat.

"Uh, Mom?"

She looked at him over her shoulder.

His face turned red. "Your dress?"

Gina sighed, raised her hand and felt the looseness at the back. She'd forgotten to zip it up. "I forgot," she said and presented her back to him. "Would you help me, please?"

His dragging footsteps across the floor told her he wasn't happy about this particular chore. She felt his fingers barely touch her back as he pulled up the zipper, then he struggled with the hook at the neck until it caught.

Gina swung around and smiled, amazed by how much he'd grown over the last year. He towered over her. Tilting her head back to meet his eyes she caught his scowl and his look of uncertainty.

"What's the matter?"

His eyes flickered over her frame. "It's a guy this time, isn't it?"

"Yes, but there's no need to worry. Okay?"

She reached up to shove a strand of shoulder-length, sandy hair behind his ear when he ducked his head, avoiding her touch. She'd been reminding herself for weeks to take him for a haircut, although she knew he'd resist. Soon it would be long enough to tie back in a ponytail. But she also knew when to choose her battles with her eldest child. Arguing with him to cut his hair was low on her list of priorities.

"Lock the door after I leave."

Jack stared at her a moment before nodding, then stepped back without uttering another word. She left the house, pausing on the steps until she heard the door lock.

It took her several times to get her engine to turn over and start up her old Honda Civic. Damn, another car wasn't in her budget—not yet—though she'd managed to put savings toward it. She was close.

Fifteen minutes later she drove past her building and found a spot two blocks away. Saturdays were busy in downtown San Antonio with all the restaurants and theaters. She walked briskly down the street until she reached a renovated building with a red brick façade. Carol Anne's Aromatherapy shop was on the main floor while Gina's business, Smooth Edges Consultations, was located above it.

She knocked on the window, waved at Carol Anne, a tall pretty blonde, then took the stairs to the second floor. She gasped and came to an abrupt halt when she reached the top step.

Stone stood beside her office door, his back against the wall. Gina moved closer, smiled at his Stetson tipped over his eyes. He appeared to be asleep on his feet.

He wore a newer, bluer pair of jeans and a clean, long-sleeved white shirt, the top left unbuttoned. His cleanliness was an improvement, but all that face hair really had to go. She could barely make out his face features. Tentatively, she reached out and touched his arm. "Mister Mitchell?"

He straightened immediately, tipped back his hat, and glanced at his watch. "You're late."

Gina gave him an apologetic smile. "Sorry about that." She unlocked her office door, stepped inside and he followed her.

His low, cool voice sent shivers down her spine when he said, "You're all dressed up."

"Just a bit," she replied, setting her purse on the desk. "I guess you could say we're on a date," she added. She *had* dressed up—even Jack had noticed. Why wouldn't Stone? Then she asked herself why, even though subconsciously she knew the answer. She hadn't been with a man in over a year. Since her husband Charlie had died. She missed a man's companionship, amongst other things, intimacy, for instance.

"A pretend date," she added quickly, seeing his frown hadn't diminished. "Since you feel you may be out of practice you could pretend I am the woman you intend to pursue."

Was that interest she saw light up his eyes?

"I like that dress," he drawled, eyes drifting lazily down her body with a masculine, appreciative look.

She hurried over to the stereo system in the corner of her office, her cheeks warm. "I brought along an assortment of music to help us get in the mood." Gina glanced at him over her shoulder, caught the gleam in his eyes and clarified her statement. "For dancing."

She held out her hand and he took it, then followed her to the center of the office. There she stopped and faced him, then placed her hand on his shoulder. He moved in close, gently took her hand, and slid his other hand around her waist.

"Ready?" she asked, her voice catching at the heated look in his eyes.

He drew her close with a big grin. "Sure am."

His beard brushed her temple. Gina had expected it to be hard and bristly and was surprised by its softness. They started dancing and within moments Stone had picked up the steps and taken the lead, which made Gina wonder just how little he knew about dancing. If she didn't know better, she'd guess he'd known how to dance all along, or he was a quick study.

She caught her breath when he suddenly swept her up into a waltz that made her head spin. He was a bit ahead of the music, even though she counted aloud, yet she couldn't fault his graceful, fluid movement. But when the music quickened, so did his steps. They weren't waltzing anymore but dancing a mean polka. Gina threw her arms around his neck when he dipped her back and her hair brushed the floor.

"Whoa, cowboy!"

Stone pulled her upright with a big grin on his lips. She kept her hands clamped around his neck and held on for dear life. Apparently, he'd forgotten the cowboy's vernacular since he didn't slow down a bit. Finally, the music ended. He stepped back and shoved his hands in his back pockets, a pleased look on his face.

"It's been so long I'd forgotten how much I enjoyed dancing, even if I wasn't very good. How'd I do, Teacher?"

Did he want the truth or some fabrication? She didn't have the heart to be angry with him, especially when he appeared to be so pleased with his performance.

"I thought we were supposed to be waltzing."

"Guess I got carried away." He stroked his beard and stared down at the floor.

Gently, she asked, "Where did you learn to dance like that?"

Because of the beard and mustache, only a small area of his skin was visible. It turned a bright shade of pink. "I told you I didn't know how."

"That's all right. I have to admit you do have natural rhythm." She offered him a brilliant smile. "Shall we try again?"

Frowning, he said, "Only if you promise not to get mad."

"I wasn't mad at you," she reassured him. "I'm *not* mad at you. But please remember that I'm leading."

"Yeah, well, that's the problem. I'm not used to being led."

No kidding. "I understand, but you must—for the present." She took his hand and moved in close. "And another thing. My feet do not leave the floor for any reason."

"I couldn't hear you over the fiddle music."

"Violin, you mean."

"Same thing."

This time Gina led, and Stone followed, within reason. Every time she exerted pressure to change direction and guide him in the steps, he fought her, not consciously she was certain, for he usually complied after an initial moment of tugging hands between them.

The thought of melting in his arms was growing more attractive by the minute, her heart thumping in double-time each time his body brushed against hers. It took all of her willpower not to lay a kiss on his lips.

She ignored her growing attraction for him, chalking her feelings up to the fact she hadn't been with a man in a long while. "This is very nice, isn't it?" He nodded and she added, "Actually, you're doing quite well."

He lifted his brow. "Think so?"

"Um-hmm."

He angled his body closer and she stiffened when his lower extremities brushed against her. "Remember what I said about leading," she reminded him.

"Right. You're the boss—for now."

Gina narrowed her eyes, wondering about his devilish smile and cryptic reply, when the shrill ringing of the telephone made them pause. Stone let go of her waist and hand and stepped back with a sigh. "I suppose you've got to answer that."

Gina nodded. "I'll just be a minute." She crossed the office and snatched up the phone on the second ring, assuming it was a work call since her boys would generally call her cell phone, until she saw her home number on the phone's display. "Hello?" After a moment, she said, "Jack? Slow down. I can't understand you when you're agitated and talking a mile a minute."

She listened again and said, "Mrs. Murray isn't home and you two are alone?"

Stone saw her eyes go round as saucers and he drew near.

"The house is on fire? Get out! Now!"

CHAPTER THREE

S tone recognized the signs of shock and noticed Gina was on the ragged edge. He took the phone from her nerveless hand and pressed her down into a chair. She sank down and closed her eyes while Stone held the phone to his ear.

"What in the hell is going on?" he growled, angry that someone had upset her, and on *his* time, no less.

Gina gasped. "That's my fifteen-year-old son!"

"Uh, sorry," he apologized. *Fifteen?* Hell, the kid had likely heard every cuss word invented by now anyway. He recalled his own colorful vocabulary during his hellish teen years. Unfortunately, some of those words were still an inherent part of his vocabulary.

He concentrated on the boy's rapid-fire explanation, his eyes lingering on Gina who seemed to have more color in her face now. He couldn't take his eyes off her beautiful brown eyes glistening with unshed tears.

"Don't worry, son," he finally said. "You did the right thing calling the police and fire department."

Stone looked away from Gina, in order to concentrate on Jack's words.

"I'll take care of your mom. Hold tight, we're on our way."

He hung up. "Fire department's already there and has put out the fire."

Gina suddenly gathered her wits, jumped from her chair, and stormed toward the door. "I've got to get home."

In two strides he caught up with her, pressed his palm above her head against the door and held it shut. "Hey, didn't you hear what I said? The fire department's contained the fire so take it easy. And your boys are just fine. You'll get there soon enough. Hell, a moment ago you looked as though you were going to keel over."

"I've never fainted in my life!"

"That may be," he said, sounding unconvinced, "but you were screaming at your boy." He stepped back and shoved his hands into his back pockets. "Then you went all quiet and turned white as a ghost."

She rolled her eyes. "Why am I standing here arguing with you?" She whirled back to the door and grabbed the doorknob, gasping when Stone's large hand covered hers.

He turned the knob and swung the door open, releasing her hand at the same time. "I'll drive you."

"I can manage on my own."

He took her keys. "You're in no condition to drive—unless you've got someone else you can call on for help. Now which one locks the door?"

He held up the keys and she pointed out the right one. He locked the door and ushered her down the stairs.

"Listen, cowboy, I know you're used to giving out orders left and right down on your ranch, but it won't work with me. Ours is strictly a business relationship. Got that?"

He nodded as he took her elbow and ushered her outside. "Business—right. After we make sure everything's okay at your house we'll get back to business."

Within moments he'd buckled her into his Bronco and drove in silence, checking on her now and again. She didn't speak but stared out the window. Fifteen minutes later they stood outside Gina's small rambler as firefighters were putting away equipment. Luckily, the fire had stayed in the kitchen area at the back of the fifties-style one story home.

Gina threw herself out of the Bronco and rushed to her boys who stood on the lawn, watching the firefighters at work. She crushed them in her arms. "Thank God you two are safe!" Sighing in relief, she eased her hold.

Jack moved completely out of her embrace and scowled at his younger brother. "Everything was fine until I fell asleep on the couch and Chris decided to play Einstein again. And Mrs. Murphy isn't answering her door. I went to her house first for help."

Gina looked at her younger son. "Honey, tell me what happened."

"I was trying to melt my old crayons to make candles," Chris replied, a sheepish look on his face. "I put them in paper cups and heated them up in the microwave, but I set the timer for too long."

She groaned, "Oh, Chris. Haven't I told you over and over again the microwave isn't to be used for anything but heating food?"

"I'm sorry, but it worked on TV. I saw it."

Stone stood a short distance away and smiled as he watched her speak to her sons. Being a single mom can't be easy, he mused. He turned to look at the back of the house and saw it had been burned clear through the walls and roof. Suddenly a car drove up and parked. Stone headed for Gina when he noticed a rotund man exiting it.

It turned out the man was an investigator from the fire department who'd been sent to question the boys. Stone arrived at Gina's side in time to hear the man say, "I'm sorry, but as soon as I get some answers from your boys, you can find a place to stay for the night. With the smoke damage, you won't be able to stay here for a while, not too long, though."

Chris explained how he'd accidentally set the fire. Jack

27

became defensive, though, when the man asked, for the second time, if either of them ever played with matches or smoked cigarettes.

"We already said no!" Jack shouted.

"Yeah. That's what they all say," the man grumbled.

Gina opened her mouth, her intentions to castigate the man for his sarcastic remark when Jack beat her to it.

"You jerk!"

Jack's face turned red as the licking flames that had burned down a portion of his house. He shoved the investigator, but Stone arrived in time to halt the man's stumbling backward steps. He steadied the man then grimaced when Jack lashed out a fist. Stone caught the punch and gave Jack a sharp warning, "Calm down. Fighting won't settle a thing."

Jack ignored Stone's warning. "Let me at the bastard!"

The fire chief scowled and turned to Gina. "I'll talk with you and your boys later, ma'am," he said meaningfully.

After he left, Stone grasped Jack's shoulders and looked him in the eyes. "Get that temper under control, son."

Jack immediately stilled, fury on his face as he yanked Stone's hands from his shoulders. "I'm not your son! Who the hell are you, anyway?"

Gina gasped. "Jack!"

"I'm a friend of your mother's."

"No, you're not. You're one of her clients."

"That, too."

"Jeez, you look like a frickin' werewolf!"

Stone let loose a ferocious growl at the top of his lungs and Jack bolted away clumsily across the grass, his long limbs out of control. Stone wondered how Gina handled the hotheaded kid without a man about. He smiled then, thinking Jack sort of reminded him of himself at that age. Unfortunately, he'd long since paid the price for losing his cool and had learned from past dire consequences to control his temper.

"Stone, I need to talk to my neighbor about what happened and why she wasn't around when the boys ran to her house."

"No problem. I'll wait here until you get back."

Gina learned that Mrs. Murphy had come down with a migraine, fell asleep and didn't hear knocking or the doorbell."

Gina reassured her things would be fine and not to worry. She also told her about the fire which made her neighbor feel even more guilty. Once Gina told her 'things happen' she left and told the woman to get some rest.

Stone turned to Gina. "I'm inviting you to stay at my ranch until your claim is settled, and your house is fixed."

"Let me think a minute," she said, her voice shaking.

Stone waited patiently as Gina bit her lip and rubbed her temples. Finally she met his gaze and heaved a sigh. "I really appreciate your offer, Mr. Mitchell, but I'm sure I'll be able to find a hotel in town."

"Nonsense. There's no sense paying for a hotel when I've plenty of room at my place."

"My insurance will cover it," she replied.

"I've heard rumblings from the firemen there's smoke damage both upstairs and down, and you don't have a back door. The firemen will board up your place once they're through here. Meanwhile you can stay with me," he insisted.

"I appreciate your kind offer, but I'm sure I'll be able to make other arrangements. Besides, like I said, your ranch is too far away from my workplace."

He frowned. "A bit over two hours is too far away?"

She nodded. "My car is ten years old and not real dependable."

"Do you have family or friends you can count on to take you in for a while?"

Gina worried her bottom lip again. "Maybe."

Two and a quarter hours later, Stone drove his Bronco beneath a wide set of wooden gates, a pleased smile on his lips. It turned out Gina's secretary hadn't answered her phone. She'd called two other friends who'd hemmed and hawed about the fact that if it were only Gina looking for a place, they'd be able to accommodate her, but they hadn't enough room for her boys. And with a big cattleman's convention in town, not a single hotel room could be found. She'd had no choice but to accept Stone's generous offer.

Luckily tomorrow was Sunday and she had no clients.

Putting aside her complaint about driving her old car this distance, they accompanied Stone and he'd drive them back and forth when she needed him to. It turned out Gina didn't work full-time days anyway, but more by appointment times she set with clients, which would help. They could mesh their schedules, he decided.

Gina had managed to pack a small bag for each of them, but still wore that sweet little black dress, Stone noticed.

After a long drive up a gravel driveway they reached a set of enormous wood gates, with a sign hanging above it that said, Falcon's Ridge Ranch. He parked in the driveway near the house and eased out of the vehicle, rubbed elbows with Jack who assisted his mother from the car. Stone ended up going around to her other side and placed a gentle hand on her waist.

She gave Jack a level look. "Don't think I've forgotten that you owe Mister Mitchell an apology."

"Like hell I do," he snarled.

"Say you're sorry right now," she snapped.

Stone was frankly astonished when Jack raised his furious red-eyed gaze to him and mumbled, "Sorry."

With a short nod, Stone acknowledged his apology, somehow guessing he hadn't meant it. Then he smiled when Jack wound an arm around his mother's shoulders. His respect for the boy soared. Family loyalty was important. He appreciated the trait since he had no close family of his own.

Stone dropped back then to walk beside the younger boy. With the beard and mustache covering much of his face, kids were usually scared of him, but not this young towhead smiling shyly up at him.

"You must have been growing that hair for a long time," Chris remarked.

Stone laughed. "You're Chris, right?"

The boy nodded.

Stone stuck out his hand as they moved up the steps. "Nice to meet you. I'm Stone Mitchell, and contrary to what your brother believes, I'm not a werewolf."

Chris grinned and sent an idolizing look at Stone.

Stone's heart clenched. Then he looked up and found his housekeeper, Marguerite Ramirez, standing squarely in the doorway.

"Hi, Marguerite, we've houseguests. This is Gina Liberatti and her sons, Jack and Chris. Gina, boys, meet Marguerite Ramirez, my housekeeper, and the best cook this side of the Mexican border."

Gina smiled, moved up another step and extended her hand. "Hello. It's nice to meet you."

A delighted grin stretched Marguerite's full lips and she reached down and eagerly grasped Gina's hand. "With a name such as yours, you are not an Americano, are you?"

"Yes, I am," Gina replied.

Stone smiled at the hesitant expression on Gina's face. Marguerite had a heart of gold but, sometimes folks didn't appreciate her candor.

"Liberatti is my maiden name. My husband's family came from Italy. But I am also half Italian, on my mother's side."

Marguerite released Gina's hand, raised her eyes to heaven and made the Sign of the Cross. "Thank you, Lord. Stoney has finally seen the light and has brought home a fine Latin-blooded woman." She looked deep into Gina's eyes and added, "A woman of great passion."

Gina blinked at the housekeeper's back as she moved into the house and then gave Stone a bewildered look, her cheeks turning red.

"I know. It's hard to know what to say," he said dryly.

Chris and Jack entered the house then.

"What does she mean?" Gina asked.

"Marguerite has this theory; if you are a 'gringo' woman, you have no passion in your soul. And passion, to her mind, is very important in man-woman relationships."

Gina frowned. "I see."

They entered the foyer. Jack immediately moved to his mother's side, casting suspicious looks at Stone.

Stone decided he'd have to do something about that. The boy didn't trust him, which was not a surprising reaction from a young boy who'd most likely had a lot of responsibility thrust upon his shoulders too early in life. Stone also knew that words alone wouldn't make the boy trust him. Then he frowned and wondered why in the hell it was so important the kid like him anyway? Jack and his mother weren't going to be permanent fixtures in his life.

Stone grinned at the young boy's wide-eyed look. The rambling ranch home with wings on two sides was topped with a red-tiled roof. The stucco had been expertly swirled in half circles and painted pale pink. The trim was shiny black and black shutters hung on either side of the numerous windows.

Stone noticed Gina taking note of the lovely Spanish tiled flooring throughout the entryway, leading into a great room with an open-style dream kitchen filled with light oak cabinets and the best of appliances. He knew the kitchen was a cook's dream.

"This is some house!" Chris shouted.

"Thanks." Stone knew he'd gone way overboard when he'd built the house, but what the hell. He'd worked his butt off to own something so wondrous, something completely his own. The big house was important to a man who'd grown up living in a one-bedroom apartment in San Antonio.

He'd been lucky in that his old Uncle Harold had given him the five-hundred-acre ranch in his will. Uncle Harold was his mom's oldest brother and he remembered meeting him the first time at fourteen, when he'd gotten into trouble with the law. Back then his mother had no idea how to handle him, a boy without a father figure; a boy who was 'hell on wheels', a troubled juvenile from twelve to fourteen. In desperation she paid a call to her brother. Harold had lost track of his young sister after she'd, as he put it, got in the family way at eighteen, yet he readily agreed to take on Stone.

After that, every summer and most weekends, Stone had been forced to work at the ranch. Initially he'd hated seeing his friends less than he wanted but with the enforced segregation he learned to enjoy being with his uncle on the ranch. Soon it seemed ranching was in his blood and he'd taken to the hard work and had found the father figure he needed in his uncle. But most importantly, he'd stayed out of trouble.

He and Uncle Harold had grown close. Stone went on to make better choices and by the time he graduated from high school, college, then police academy and finally ranger schooling he was a responsible twenty-seven-year old.

He spent the next three years as a ranger, then was shot and injured. Shortly after being released from the hospital, he was called by Harold's lawyer, informing him he'd passed on. Stone was stunned he'd inherited the spread, with four-hundred head of Brahman cattle, a few milk cows, sheep, chickens and horses. He'd been able to bypass ranching 101, due to his experience in working the ranch all those years.

Marguerite stopped in the middle of the kitchen and raised her brow. "How long will Mrs. Liberatti be staying?"

"Awhile," Stone replied.

"Just overnight," Gina said at the same time.

Marguerite looked between the two of them and folded her plump arms over her matronly bosom. "So, which is it?"

Stone shrugged. "We'll talk about it later."

"You boys hungry?" Marguerite asked, turning her attention to Jack and Chris.

They nodded.

"I can imagine since it's almost 8:00 p.m. I've plenty of enchiladas and tacos so Marguerite will feed you."

"Hope you like Mexican food," Stone said as he took Gina's elbow and guided her to an oversized wood trestle table surrounded by several chairs. "It's Marguerite's specialty, which is one of the reasons I hired her. Can't get enough of that hot, spicy stuff."

She smiled. "I love Mexican food." She sank into a chair Stone had pulled out for her across from her boys who'd already settled in.

Nodding his approval, Stone said, "You'll stay until your settlement comes through and your house has been repaired."

Gina raised her brow. "I beg your pardon?"

"Didn't you say all of your family lives out of town?"

"Yes, but there are plenty of hotels and motels in San Antonio, and the convention only lasts a few days. Besides, driving to work and back, two hours each way, isn't appealing, not that I'm not grateful for the accommodations for the night."

"I can't do much about the commute, but you're welcome to stay as long as you like. Besides, we'll have more time to work on my improvements."

"Figured there was an ulterior motive." She laughed, bit her lip, her expression thoughtful. "Thank you."

He moved to the end spot on her right and took a seat, his elbows on the table, hands clasped as he looked at each of them. He liked this feeling of 'family' and could get used to it, he decided. He grinned when he watched Gina's sons eyeing the food but had manners each to wait to begin eating.

Vibrant-colored Fiesta stoneware, each place setting a different color, graced the table. The water glasses were tall and narrow. Gleaming copper clad-bottomed pans were hanging from hooks above the stove. Gina sighed.

"Eat up," Stone said, grinning at Gina. "The way your boys are shoveling in the food you won't get a single taco if you don't grab a couple now."

"These are the best tacos I ever tasted," said Jack as he scooped a heaping spoonful of refried beans onto his plate. "Beans too."

Marguerite arched her brows and looked at Gina. "Hollow legs, no?"

Gina rolled her eyes. "You can't even begin to imagine." She frowned when Jack snatched up the half-gallon carton of milk and poured another glass, his third since she'd taken a seat at the table.

"Jack—"

"He's a growing boy," Stone inserted with an indulgent smile. "I can afford the cow."

Jack turned a skeptical look on Stone but didn't utter a word as he set down the carton of milk.

Gina ate two tacos and a small helping of refried beans. When she finished she carried her plate to the counter. "I'll help you clean up, Marguerite."

The older woman shrugged. "I've never been one to turn down an offer in the kitchen."

"Ha!" Stone exclaimed. "You shove me out the door whenever I so much as pick up a plate."

"That's because whenever you touch one with those big paws of yours you break it. Why don't you take the boys on a short tour of the ranch? Maybe they'd like to see the horses. It's too late for much more than that."

"Horses?" Jack asked with thinly veiled interest.

Stone frowned at Marguerite. "You're trying to get rid of me."

"You're imagining things. I'd just like to get to know Mrs. Liberatti is all," his housekeeper replied.

"You mean you want to exchange gossip with her." Stone shoved back his chair and came to his feet. "Come on upstairs, boys. I'll show you the rooms you'll be occupying before we head out to tour the barn."

"All right!" said Jack, with more enthusiasm than Gina had heard from him in a long time.

"Only for the night," Gina corrected him.

They ignored her as they followed Stone out of the kitchen. As Gina dried a plate, she heard their steps on the stairs. She nearly dropped the plate when Marguerite asked, "He's some man, no?"

CHAPTER FOUR

Too much man!

Gina knew she wasn't anywhere near ready for a man-woman relationship again. Relationships went right along with accountability and commitment. Her boys were responsibility enough without adding a man into the equation.

"You want him, you must go after him."

"But I don't want him," Gina protested.

"Bah! I see it in your eyes when you look at him, and I see it in his eyes when he looks at you. But you are both fools."

"And why is that?"

"Because you are fighting against what only fate can decide."

Gina narrowed her eyes. "You believe we are destined to be together?"

Marguerite nodded.

"I'm sorry to disappoint you, but ours is a business relationship, nothing more. Good grief, we've only just met."

"He came to you for advice on making improvements in himself so that he may catch himself a wife, didn't he?"

Gina nodded.

"Well, you'll soon find there isn't much to change in Stoney."

Once he shaves off the beard and trims his hair, maybe, and cleaned up his penchant for swearing. "I'm teaching him to dance," Gina said.

"He might need some help with that," Marguerite conceded. "What else did he ask you to help him change?"

"Assist him in selecting new clothing. He'll need a new suit or two once he begins courting. A woman appreciates a man in a suit. I know I do." Then she thought of him in his blue jeans and chambray shirt and thought he looked pretty darned good in those too, dirt and all, and a size too small.

Marguerite grinned. "He has suits, the kind with all the fine seams across the shoulders and down the front and back."

"Western cut, you mean?" Gina said, unable to hide her interest. *The kind that nipped in at the waist and would emphasize his broad shoulders.*

The housekeeper nodded and rolled her eyes. "But let me tell you, my old heart pounds like the thundering hooves of rampaging cows when he wears his suit made of the finest, softest black leather."

Gina caught her breath. "Did you say…leather?"

The image of Stone's slim hips, trim buttocks and muscular thighs encased in a pair of soft, clinging leather pants made her heart race—until his beastly visage entered her mind.

Marguerite nodded. "Come on and I'll show you, although I admit the suit's a lot more interesting on Stone than hanging in the closet."

"Stop! I believe you." Gina's laughter bubbled forth, halting the housekeeper in her tracks.

"What makes me curious is that he agreed to go shopping at all," Marguerite said, shaking her head. "He detests shopping."

Gina shrugged. "He suggested it. He'll also need to purchase some looser fitting jeans rather than the skin-tight, revealing…" Gina covered her hot cheeks with her palms and met Marguerite's knowing smile.

"Uh-huh. Like I said. Wait till you see him in his leather pants."

Gina gulped. Then they burst into laughter as they walked arm in arm into the family room with their cups of coffee. Gina couldn't recall if she'd ever grown more comfortable with a human being as quickly as she had with Marguerite. Gina sat on the sofa and placed her cup on the coffee table while Marguerite settled her bulk into a chair across from her.

Gina said, "Is Stone his given name?"

Marguerite shook her head. "It's Stryker."

Another unusual name. "Why did he change it?"

"He didn't. His mama used to say his body was hard as stone, and that he possessed a stubborn disposition, besides, so the name stuck. He's a fine man. You won't find none better."

"I believe you." Gina had to admit she didn't know of anyone who would so willingly take a complete stranger into his home.

A short while later, Marguerite announced, "Well, I gotta get home. By the way, in case the two new boys arrive before I get here just let them in and tell Stone." Marguerite struggled to her feet and headed for the front door.

Gina scrambled off the sofa and followed her. "What boys?"

Marguerite paused at the door. "Didn't Stone tell you anything about himself, except for wanting to find a wife?"

Gina shook her head.

"Well, before Stoney got into ranching, he got...well, I'd better let him tell you about it." Marguerite glanced at the clock on the wall. "Like I said, I've got to get home so I'll see you in the morning."

Gina returned to the family room. She sank down onto the sofa and reached for the television remote, thinking over Marguerite's revelations about Stone. *What a man was right!*

Stone's long stride easily kept pace with Jack and Chris as they moved toward the house. As they reached the back door, Stone said, "Shoes off. There's no telling what you might have stomped in."

He toed off his boots while they removed their tennis shoes. "Want a snack?"

"Yes, sir!" Chris shouted. Jack merely nodded.

Stone had learned Gina's oldest son, Jack, was the serious, thoughtful son while Chris was happy go-lucky and easier to read. Stone found he was drawn to the twelve-year old.

"Are those real snakeskin?" Chris stared in awe at Stone's boots parked next to the door.

"Sure are." Stone took in their well-worn athletic shoes. "Don't you boys own a pair of boots?"

"Mom can't afford them as long as my feet keep growing," Jack said defensively, his face turning pink. "When we first moved to Texas, I had a pair of boots. Red ones. Wouldn't wear red now, but I sure do like yours."

"These are pretty old, but they're broke in the way I like them. There's nothing worse than getting used to a new pair of boots. I'll have to see about buying each of you a pair."

They looked at Stone in surprise.

"Can't be helping me out at Falcon's Ridge without boots now, can you?" Stone scowled down at their worn shoes. "Besides, how do you expect to ride a horse in those?"

Chris whooped at this news.

"It won't be a problem since *we* won't be staying, and *they* won't be riding."

Three heads whipped around to the family room where Gina stood framed in the doorway, hands on her curvy hips.

Stone realized she must have been sleeping. Her eyes were drowsy, her hair a tumbled mass around her shoulders and her skirt was wrinkled. His gaze lowered and focused on her elegant bare feet. Then he looked up and met the snapping look in her eyes.

"Didn't Marguerite show you to your room before she left?" She shook her head and he said, "I'll remedy that right now. I'm sure you'd like to change into something more comfortable."

Her face turned pink. "I haven't a change of clothing with me so I'll sleep in my dress, I guess." She turned to her sons. "Time for bed."

"But, Mom, it's only nine o'clock," Jack protested.

"Oh." She sighed. "I thought it was later. Wash up then and you may watch TV for another hour or so. We'll be leaving early in the morning."

"There's a television in each of your rooms," Stone said, smiling at the relieved expressions on their faces. He also remembered when 'bedtime' was an evil word. "Your mom and I need to settle a few things, in private."

Suspicion rose in Jack's face. "Do you want me to stay, Mom?"

Stone folded his arms and widened his stance but remained silent as he stared between mother and son. Jack's protective attitude was commendable but growing tiresome.

"No, I'm fine." Gina wound an arm around each boy's shoulders and hugged them tight. Stone hid a grin behind his hand when he noticed their pained expressions.

After they left the kitchen Stone pinned his gaze on Gina. "Be reasonable. Of course you're staying longer than tonight."

"You seem to forget that ours is a business arrangement. We're not staying, and my sons are not riding."

Stone just smiled.

Gina scowled. "I'm dead serious about this, Mister Mitchell."

His smile slipped. "They'll be safe with me."

"They've never ridden before!"

He just shrugged. "There's a first time for everything."

"I'll think about it."

With a grin he took her elbow and guided her down the hallway. Then he stopped outside an open door and swept his arm with a flourish. "So, will this do?"

Gina's eyes widened as she looked into a bedroom that had been painted a bright sunny yellow. A big brass bed, draped with a yellow and blue floral comforter, was centered against one wall. A small bedside table with a lace tablecloth, and a pine dresser with an oval mirror hanging on the wall above it, completed the charming bedroom furnishings.

"I'll find something for you to wear to bed."

She swept her hair back from her forehead and gave him a wry look. "Okay."

After he left Gina flopped down on the bed and threw her arms over her head. Staring at the ceiling she thought about her new client and the job of smoothing his rugged edges. She wondered what in the world she'd gotten herself into.

Closing her eyes, she thought back fifteen and a half years ago to her wedding day. It hadn't been happy as far as wedding days went. She'd been a naïve seventeen-year old who'd just graduated from high school. Her husband, Charlie, had only been nineteen, in his second year of college and far from being ready for marriage.

She'd had just two dates with Charlie Benton when she gave up her virginity to him. To her surprise and dismay, she soon discovered she was pregnant. Her father had given them no choice but to marry.

Gina had loved her husband, and he had loved her, but theirs wasn't a grand passion. And over the years, they'd developed a mutual respect for each other. But most importantly, he'd been a means of escaping her dictatorial father, though he had through the years become somewhat controlling too. *Men.*

"Here you go."

Surprised, she lurched up, walked to the doorway, and reached for the long-sleeved white shirt Stone held out for her. She slipped her arms into the sleeves, which were too long so she rolled back the cuffs.

"Is it okay?" he asked tentatively.

"Yes, fine, thanks." She tipped her head back and stared at him, her heart pounding at the smoldering look in his eyes. That look made her distinctly uncomfortable, and she started having second thoughts about spending the night. "It isn't right that we inconvenience you like this."

"You're not. By the way, is there a chance we can continue where we left off with the dance lesson tomorrow?"

She smiled. "Of course. Normally I don't work Sundays but will make an exception for you, as long as we're staying here."

"Hell, we could probably add Sundays to work on the dancing, too. The sooner I learn the better."

He grinned and folded his arms across his chest as he leaned a shoulder against the doorjamb. "So, tell me, what do you do, instead, on Sundays?"

"We attend church, usually eleven o'clock Mass. Then we eat lunch at Smiley's Café. In my sons' opinion, they make the greatest ham and eggs, not to mention the world's best baking powder biscuits. Afterward, we usually take in a movie, or play a game or two of pool at home."

Stone nodded. "Sounds good." He turned and headed for the door, pausing, and smiling at her over his shoulder. "Would you mind if I joined you for lunch some Sunday?"

"I wouldn't mind." As soon as the agreeable words slipped from her lips, she wondered why she'd said them.

"Good night, Gina."

As he closed the door, she caught the amusement in his dark eyes then looked away as heat seeped into her cheeks. The man simply was too persuasive, though she admitted it hadn't taken much persuasion to accept his invite.

She removed the shirt, then her dress and bra, left her underwear and donned the shirt again, catching his spicy, masculine scent wafting through the room. She marveled at how he'd managed to maneuver himself into her life so easily. Okay, so it was only lunch on Sunday, but somehow, she had a feeling he wouldn't stop at that. She had a strong hunch he'd appear on her doorstep every Sunday if she allowed him the opportunity.

There was something about him that made her think he was a loner, by choice, but now the 'loner' was lonesome and looking for a mate by Christmas. Thinking about her first impressions of him, she decided he was likable, courteous, and handsome, in a rugged way.

He appeared to have been blessed with an easy-going disposition, but she couldn't ignore the fact he'd revealed his stubborn nature and seemed to be too strong-willed for her taste.

Long ago she'd vowed, if the opportunity presented itself, to never become involved with another controlling man. Living with her father, then Charlie, had cured her. But she also couldn't deny that she was drawn to Stone's charismatic personality, which made him as lethal as a rattler's bite.

She hated snakes. Yet, as she tucked herself beneath the sheets, she had a feeling she'd eagerly accept a bite from him.

CHAPTER FIVE

Gina spent the night tossing and turning. Upon waking to a quiet house, she rose and tiptoed down the hallway. Once she located Stone, the priority of the day would be retrieving clothes from her house since she'd decided to stay at least another night or two. There was no sense exposing her children to the stench of a smoky motel, which was about all she could afford at the moment. She made a mental note to herself to call her insurance company in the morning.

She peered into the kitchen and found only Marguerite sitting at the table, a cup of coffee at her elbow as she read the newspaper.

"Good morning," Gina said.

Marguerite looked up and smiled. "You sleep well?"

"Once I finally managed to fall asleep." She glanced at the clock and gasped. "I hadn't realized it was so late."

Marguerite shrugged. "Your sons slept in, too. The only one up when I arrived this morning was Stone. You won't find a harder working man."

"I can believe that." Gina crossed the kitchen, pulled a cup from a hook, and poured a cup of coffee. She inhaled the fragrant aroma and took a sip as she leaned back against the counter. "I gather Mister Mitchell is out and about already?"

"Since five."

A horrified expression crossed Gina's face. "My Lord, that's the middle of the night, isn't it?"

Marguerite chuckled. "Ranchers have many chores to do. The earlier in the day they finish them the better. Once the sun rises, it's much too hot to work outside. He came back around eight, had breakfast and then headed out again. Your boys are with him now, in the corral on the east side of the house."

Gina's eyes widened. "My sons were up by eight on a weekend?"

"Oh, they were eager to get into the corral with the horses. Stone's giving them a riding lesson."

Gina choked on her coffee and smacked her cup down on the counter.

"That oldest son of yours will be a fine horseman some day. Of course, once Chris gets over his fear of them, he'll be okay."

Gina ran for the door.

"Now where do you think you're going?"

"I didn't give Stone permission to teach them to ride."

"Well, you can't go out there dressed like—"

Gina missed Marguerite's grin as she tore outside.

———

Stone sat on the fence, his legs hooked under a rail, arms braced, Chris beside him. He trained his gaze on Jack, who sat on one of his quarter horses and cantered around the perimeter of the corral. Shortly after Jack had swung up into the saddle and followed his directions, Stone immediately saw he was a natural. Unlike Chris who still hadn't done much more than pet the horse's muzzle. Jack, on the other hand, was fearless and a bit reckless.

Over the past hour, Stone had corrected the boy, reminding him time and again to take it slow and easy. He didn't want to even think about the possibility of him getting hurt, for that would mean dealing with his overprotective mother.

Chris tugged on Stone's sleeve. "Think I'll get a snack."

Stone grinned. He must be growing because eating was all he seemed to think about. "Go for it, son."

His eyes tracked Chris as he ran toward the house. When he reached the back door, Gina stepped out. Chris stood directly in front of her, blocking Stone's view, with the exception of her pretty face and shoulders. She reached out a hand and Chris backed away, shoving his hair off his forehead.

Chris's body language said it all. *I'm not a baby anymore.*

Gina dropped her hand to her side while she spoke to Chris. Stone had caught the momentary pang of regret on her face when Chris had shied away from her touch. Stone couldn't miss the longing in her expression to reach out and embrace the boy, but he knew Chris wouldn't welcome her physical touch much longer. Embraces from mom were too embarrassing by his age.

Stone imagined her with another child—a baby—cradled in her arms; imagined her nursing him or her at her breast. Yes, the woman needed another child. *His child.* Then he scowled and wondered where in the hell that idea came from. Gina was hardly his type. *Who was he kidding?* He had a feeling she was more his type than he was hers. He narrowed his eyes on her curves, cursing softly when he saw her slim, bare legs eating up the ground as she headed toward him.

"Damn," he breathed, taking in her state of undress.

Never would he have imagined Gina to be an exhibitionist, but now she strode toward him, wearing only his shirt, tails flapping in the breeze. She'd left the shirt open midway down the front, and with each step she took he caught glimpses of creamy cleavage.

His eyes drifted lower. He noticed how the tails afforded him fleeting glimpses of silky white panties. Her slim legs were sleek in the sunlight, and her dainty feet were bare as she picked her way across the lawn. Then he looked up and saw her thinned lips and narrowed eyes. She'd been insecure yesterday about the boys learning how to ride, and he meant to find out the reason. From the ticked off look on her face, he figured she'd tell him, too.

Her hair hung loose over her shoulders as though she'd just tumbled out of bed. Her face had been scrubbed free of makeup, which was fine with him. Make-up would only cover up her natural beauty. He hopped down from the fence when she reached his side. He was beginning to think Rachel Williams was a pale comparison to Gina Liberatti.

She stopped abruptly in front of him, arms crossed as she tapped one bare foot and scowled. "What do you think you're doing? Wasn't I clear last night?"

"You mean about the boys learning how to ride?" He settled his hands on his hips and added, "Don't worry, they're doing fine."

She swept her bangs off her forehead and his eyes riveted on the sheen of perspiration there. "Obviously, you have selective hearing. Let me tell you something, Mister Mitchell. My husband climbed the tallest mountains, raced the fastest cars, and parachuted out of airplanes with little thought for his family and his own safety. And before I forget, he also bungee-jumped from a fifty-story building, not once, but twice!"

"O-kay," Stone replied, waiting for her to finish.

"The thing about all of his dare-devil tactics was that he wasn't any good at them. He broke more bones in his body during our marriage than a hundred people ever could in a lifetime, but nothing stopped him. It's ironic that his career, not his penchant for thrill seeking, ended his life."

"Jack told me he was stationed on an oil rig in the gulf."

"That's right. He was an engineer with Aimes Oil and had been offered his choice of places to work. He'd always imagined himself living and working in Texas, even though we both were born and raised in the state of Washington."

"Folks are attracted to Texas for one reason or another. We've lots to offer."

"Hey, Stone."

Stone turned and found Jack walking toward them, leading his horse by the reins. "How'd I do?"

"Great." He hooked an arm around Jack's neck and pulled him close. Jack grinned up at him then turned to his mother as he eased away from Stone. Jack swept a critical look over his mother and his face reddened.

While Jack was obviously shocked and embarrassed by his mother's state of undress, Stone wasn't. Hell, he liked her this way, yet he sympathized with Jack and tried to find some way to end this humiliating moment. What was ironic and incredible was the fact Gina seemed completely unaware that she'd left the house with little on. And then he damned himself for not telling her as soon as she reached him.

"What's wrong, honey?" Gina asked. "Are you ill?"

She reached out to touch Jack's forehead, but he backed away.

"I'm hungry. See you." He whirled around and ran for the house.

Gina shook her head, puzzled. "What's gotten into him? I hope he isn't getting sick again. It took him a long time to recover from mononucleosis last winter, and—"

She stopped talking and her eyes narrowed on the growing smile Stone couldn't control.

"Jack getting sick isn't amusing."

"No." He sputtered then burst into outright laughter.

Gina scowled and crossed her arms over her breasts. "What in the world is so funny?"

His laughter faded as he swept her body with a long look, a wicked gleam in his eyes. She followed the direction of his gaze, caught her breath, and clutched her middle. She dropped both hands and unsuccessfully tried covering her thighs. She gave up, swiveled on her bare feet, and stalked away.

Stone cursed and went after her, unable to resist staring at her lush rear swishing side to side. What a woman! When he drew close, he grasped her elbow and spun her around to face him, schooling his face into a contrite expression, but it wasn't easy. "I'm sorry," he said gently. "I should have warned you sooner, but you didn't give me a chance."

Gina slammed her eyes shut, fisted her hands at her sides and counted to ten.

He released her arms and circled her, checking her over from head to toe. His grin widened when she moved right along with him, turning in an effort to keep her front side to him. Finally, with a laugh, he grasped her shoulders.

"Now, hold still a minute." He looked down over her shoulder. "Besides, it's not as though you're bare-butt—"

"Don't say it!" Gina shrieked as she pulled out of his grasp. "For goodness sake, your employees could have been out and about and seen me like this."

"Employees?" He raised his brow. "They're called hands, and they don't work weekends."

As luck would have it Stone looked up at the sound of tires on the driveway. "Damn," he muttered as one of his hands, Johnny Winery, parked his pickup truck in the middle of the driveway, jumped out and headed his way. He turned to Gina hiding behind him, digging her fingernails into his forearm.

"Oh, no! What am I going to do?"

Moving in front of her, he muttered, "You're just a bitty thing so walk behind me, and I'll shadow you. Once I meet up with Johnny, I'll distract him so you can make a run for the house."

She did precisely as he suggested, staying in his shadow, nearly bumping into his broad back when he met up with Johnny.

"Hey there, friend," Stone said jovially, extending his hand. "What brings you out this way on such a fine morning?"

Gina backed away, grateful for Johnny's and her own small

stature. When she felt the first step of the stairs against the back of her heel she swiveled around and took them two at a time.

She stormed into the kitchen and came to a skidding halt in the doorway. Marguerite stood at the counter, chopping onions, tears running down her face. The older woman gave her an innocent smile, yet Gina couldn't miss the satisfied look in her eyes.

"Why didn't you stop me from leaving the house half dressed?"

Marguerite swiped at her tears with the edge of her apron. "Stoney got a real good look at you, didn't he?"

"Yes! I wish you'd said something."

"What did Stoney say?" Marguerite asked.

"Bah, that male chauvinist? Not much, but he couldn't keep his eyes off me."

"Ah." Marguerite breathed, a big smile wreathing her face. "So, you've gained his attention. That's good—very good."

Gina gave an impotent shriek and stalked out of the kitchen with Marguerite's boisterous laughter ringing in her ears.

CHAPTER SIX

M onday morning dawned hot and muggy; one of those days where clothes stuck to the body.

Gina hadn't been too lucky in life so far. Why should this day, a few days after her house had caught fire, be different than any other? She'd learned this morning that every hotel and motel in the San Antonio area had been booked for another convention for the next four days. Oh, the staff at each hotel she called told her the reservations had been made long ago so she wouldn't have gotten in anyway. They didn't know what to say when she asked them why they hadn't told her about two conventions back to back in the first place when she'd first called to make a reservation.

She also learned who her true friends in her life weren't! None of them wanted to have her and her boys camped out for any length of time. Stone's offer was a generous one and she really had no choice but to take him up on it.

After she'd made her calls to reschedule client appointments until the following week, Stone had driven her to her house. There she'd packed more clothing and personal items she and her sons would require for their longer stay—until rooms were available at one of the hotels, which looked to be Monday of next week at the soonest. Everything smelled like smoke so she'd be busy over the next few days washing clothes, but at least they hadn't burnt up in the fire.

After supper Gina returned to her room to unpack her clothes when she heard angry male voices from down the hall. She rushed from the bedroom and skidded to a halt in the open doorway of Jack's room. Jack had Chris pinned to the bed in a headlock any pro-wrestler would envy.

Gina watched them a moment, enjoying their wrestling with a faint smile on her lips, happy that they were happy. She frowned. Upon closer inspection Jack had a grimace of a smile on his face and Chris's was turning scarlet from Jack's hold. She scrambled across the carpet, reached down and yanked Jack off his brother.

"What's going on?" she snapped.

Jack plunked down on the side of the bed, his lips in a mutinous line.

Chris looked at his mother, tears in his eyes. "Jack's mad at me."

Gina raised her brow. "No kidding? The hundred-dollar question is why?" She stared at Jack.

Her eldest gave her a cool, long look from the tip of her naked toes to the top of her head without replying. Heat crept into her face as his disdain, reminding her she still wasn't properly dressed. But she was decent. Her white terry cloth bathrobe covered her to her knees.

She held his eyes with as much authority as she could muster, crossed her arms, and waited.

Finally, he said, "Chris thought it would be real nice if you married Mister Mitchell and gave us a new daddy. I told him I don't want another daddy. Though I wouldn't mind living on this ranch," he added.

Stone chose that precise moment to appear. His eyes narrowed on Gina then they settled on the boys huddled on opposite ends of the bed.

"Is there a problem?" he asked.

Gina said, "A small one, but we're working it out."

"I'm heading out to the barn to milk cows. You guys said you were interested in watching. You two coming?" Stone asked the boys.

"Sure thing," Jack replied, hopping off the bed. He headed for the door, but Gina blocked him from leaving. She looked at Stone. "We've unfinished business. They'll be along shortly."

Stone stared at her a moment, nodded, then left, leaving Gina standing toe to toe with Jack.

"Sit down, please," Gina said, pointing at the bed.

Jack gave her another mutinous look before storming back to the bed. He sank down and scowled at the floor.

Gina closed the bedroom door and sat down between them. "Listen, honey," she said, turning to Chris. "As much as you—all of us—like Mister Mitchell I've no intentions of marrying him. I'm sorry. He's simply a client, nothing more."

Chris's face crumpled. Gina sighed and wound her arm around him.

Jack came to his feet and grasped one of Chris's shoulders. "It's the three of us from now on, bro. Get used to it." Jack gave his mother a pointed look. "May I leave?"

"Apologize to Chris first."

Jack's lips thinned but then he turned to his brother. "Sorry, Chris," he muttered. "See you outside."

Gina flinched when he slammed the door. Jack's surly mood frazzled her, and she wondered if it were possible for teenaged boys to have PMS.

She smiled at Chris. "I know you miss your daddy, but you know it wouldn't be right for me to marry someone I didn't love because you'd like a new daddy, would it?"

"But I like it here!" Chris cried, "Even if I'm scared of the horses. I'll get used to them. Stone said I would, and he said I could help him chop wood to stock up for the winter starting tomorrow.

And he's going to show us how to fix fences, milk his cows and feed his chickens. I've wanted to learn how to use tools for a long time, but every time I pick up any of dad's stuff you tell me I need to have someone teach me how to use them first. But who'll teach me?"

From the corner of her eye, Gina saw movement. She turned, saw Stone standing in the open doorway again, an expectant look on his face.

"We're ready to head out." He smiled down at Chris. "You coming?"

Chris grinned and hopped from the bed. "Yes!" he shouted, then ran beneath Stone's arm and scooted out the door.

Gina looked at Stone who'd braced his hands on the door's framework a few inches above his head, his big body taking up most of the space. She narrowed her eyes and wondered how the devil he'd opened the door without making a sound.

"He's right, you know. How about I show him how to use those tools?"

She prayed he hadn't heard Chris's comments about marriage. "For the short while we're here its fine, I guess. Thanks for offering."

"No problem. They're good boys, Gina, and you've done a great job raising them on your own since their dad passed on. Think about staying longer, won't you?"

"We can't stay. If you can drive us home next Monday, I'll appreciate it."

"Of course." He started to leave, then paused and looked at her over his shoulder. "If you change your mind my door's always open."

After he left, Gina felt more confused than ever. She was delighted her sons were happy and comfortable with Stone, but resentful that a stranger appeared to have so much influence over them. Not wanting to grow too fond of him, she decided she couldn't allow him to become a permanent fixture in their lives.

A short while later Gina, dressed in blue jeans and tank top with an old pair of tennis shoes, and sat between Stone and Chris on the fence as Jack cantered inside the corral.

Stone had just returned on his horse, along with several of his hands to whom he'd introduced her. The hands left for home then.

Then Jack maneuvered his horse over to them. The day had turned hot, but the sun beating down on Gina's bare head felt wonderful. The heat didn't bother her as it did some folks. She decided it must be because of her northwest upbringing where for so many months of the year folks longed for light and warmth instead of clouds and rain.

She jumped, startled when Jack's horse butted his head against her shoulder. She smiled and stroked his nose.

"So, when can I ride outside the ring, Stone?"

Gina had given up on the boys calling him Mr. Mitchell, especially since Stone insisted on the less formal first name basis.

"I'd say you're ready now. If your mom says it's okay, we'll take a ride out to the east end of my property line. I've a herd of cattle out there I need to check on."

Man and boy turned to Gina with expectant looks on their faces. She sighed. "Well, all right, but be careful, Jack."

"Thanks, Mom. I will."

"I'm not at all secure about this."

Stone smiled. "Which brings me to my next request; I've a horse I can ride with a double saddle. Chris could join us."

Chris's downcast expression diminished. "Can I?" he asked, hope in his eyes.

The look on Chris's face made Gina cave. "I suppose so," she said reluctantly.

Stone nudged Chris in the side with his elbow. "Why don't you guys head on in and take care of business before we leave. We could be gone for a couple hours."

Chris gave a whoop and ran into the house. Jack dismounted, tied up his horse to a fence post and tore after his brother.

Gina followed them but stopped and looked at Stone in surprise when he said, "You could come too if you want."

"I don't think so, but thanks."

"I'd be with you all the way, and we'd take it slow. I've got Millie, a real gentle mare you'll like. By the way, how come you've been living in Texas all these years and haven't learned to ride?"

Gina's heart raced at the sultry look on his face, but she managed to say, "Just never had the chance, I guess."

Ironically, her dare-devil husband tried all sorts of dangerous activities for the thrill but never mentioned horseback riding.

"Let me know if you change your mind about coming along."

Oh, but the man knew how to put on the pressure. Gina's boys tore out of the house, ran past her and Stone followed them into the barn. She followed slowly, apprehension and excitement tingling up her spine. If she hadn't spent the past nine years worrying about her husband's antics, maybe she wouldn't be so scared about her sons trying new things. An idea entered her mind then as she watched Stone tighten the cinch on his horse's underbelly.

"You might be able to change my mind about riding."

He gave her a sidewise look. "Is that a fact?"

"I'm willing to try, if you'll make an appointment with a barber."

He shrugged. "I'm game."

Her jaw gaped. "So, you'll have your hair trimmed and shave off your mustache and beard?"

"Just the hair trim."

"But—"

She saw his jaw tighten as he added, "I'm attached to my whiskers. I've already told you I'm not getting rid of them."

She stared at him, wondering why he was being so stubborn, then Chris spoke up, a slight tremble in his voice.

"I think I can ride on my own."

Stone grinned. "Okay, Chris, pull out Rusty, that little palomino, will you? He's saddled and ready to go."

"Sure thing!" Chris said.

Gina caught the excitement in Chris' voice and his ecstatic expression made her smile.

"Jack, go on out and mount Jasper."

"Yes!" Jack shouted and ran out of the barn.

Stone watched Chris approach the stall, open the door, carefully took up Rusty's reins and tentatively pulled him from the stall and outside.

Then Stone led his horse outside, and Gina slowly ambled behind him. Darn but she wanted to join them. She'd wanted to try riding ever since they'd moved to Texas. With Stone at her side she felt fairly confident she'd succeed. Maybe settling for the haircut would be a wise move—for the moment.

"I've changed my mind," she announced.

Stone's left foot was in the stirrup. He narrowed his eyes on her. "You're sure?"

"I—I think so," she murmured nervously, eyeing his horse.

"Good. We'll ride double."

She nodded, relieved that she wouldn't have to manage on her own.

Stone smiled and he pulled his foot out of the stirrup, reached up and yanked the saddle off, then handed her the reins to his horse, Midnight. "Just pull him out of the barn for me. It'll be easier to saddle him outside with the double saddle." After handing her the reins he strode over to a back wall where saddles were located.

"All right, Mom!" Chris shouted, appearing in the doorway on Rusty.

Jack appeared next to Chris on Jasper. "Stone? Can we go ahead and start out?"

"Walking only," Stone ordered as he moved inside the barn again.

"Yes, sir," both boys said in unison before they headed slowly down the driveway.

She nodded as she bit her lip, grabbed the reins tightly and led

Midnight carefully outside, staying far away from him. She was scared he'd step on her. Then she started thinking about sharing a saddle with him and sighed. She had nothing to worry about she finally decided since he'd been the perfect gentleman.

But as she thought on how he'd interfered in her phone call at the office, and how he'd maneuvered her into staying at his ranch, and the incident yesterday morning when she'd left his house nearly naked. Okay, so maybe he was on the grayer shade of white with regards to gentlemanly behavior. His slightly controlling nature was a bit bothersome, but she'd pegged him now and would be on her guard.

He returned from the barn with a huge saddle over his shoulder with two seats and a small backrest behind each seat and a rifle in his hand.

"Why the gun?" she asked in surprise.

He propped it against the slatted corral fence. "You've been living here long enough to know lots of folks carry guns in Texas—just in case." He threw the saddle over the horse's back and cinched it in place.

"In case of what?"

"Don't worry." He snatched up the rifle and jammed it into the scabbard at the back of his saddle. As he swung onto his horse, he held out his hand to assist her. "Just put your foot in the stirrup there."

"I said, in case of what?" She crossed her arms and gave him a mutinous look.

He dropped his hand with a sigh. "There's all sorts of wildlife around these parts, most of it pretty tame. Are you coming?"

"I suppose," she said, unwilling to be left behind. She was thankful she wore a pair of trendy stretch jeans for she was able to raise her leg high and place her foot in the stirrup ahead of the one his foot rested in. She gasped in surprise when he hauled her easily up in front of him and she settled into the seat. "What do I hold onto?" she asked.

"The pommel's okay."

She latched onto it and he leaned forward, surrounding her waist with his right hand, the stirrups in the left.

"Feel safe now?" he murmured.

She nodded briskly and he chuckled.

She gasped when he kicked the horse's sides and they bounced down the road. Within moments they caught up with Jack and Chris.

After a while, Gina gave up trying to keep her spine straight and relaxed against Stone's broad chest. The pleasant scent of sandalwood from where he sat behind her filled her senses with erotic thoughts. His scent was clean, smooth with a bit of roughness, which appealed to her.

"That's better," he murmured into her ear, nearly melting in sweet bliss when his nose rubbed against her neck and she closed her eyes and took a deep breath, then expelled it.

She straightened when the boys ambled alongside them. Then he guided the boys along a fence-line as he explained the workings of the ranch. Much of the land was flat, and the grass was dry and brown. Now and again he'd point out a herd in the distance.

"I'm amazed by the size of your spread," Gina said.

"It's actual mid-sized, around 500 acres. My neighbor, Rachel Williams' Rockin' J is three times larger."

Gina understood why the widow Williams might be attractive to Stone. His spread, once he joined with hers would be huge.

Stone dismounted, tossed his horse's reins over and around the railing and Chris followed suit. Reaching up, he easily settled his big hands around Gina's waist and lifted her down to the ground.

Was it her imagination that he stood there a moment, his head tilted, meeting her eyes in an appreciative gaze until she stepped back with a nervous smile. The man was potent with the black Stetson on his head, the worn jeans and black t-shirt stretched across his mountainous shoulders.

Then they moved closer to the broken stretch of electric barbed wire fencing. Gina stood a short distance away from Stone and her sons. They were discussing what supplies they'd need to fix the fence in the morning.

Luckily, school had ended two weeks ago, a good thing considering her current housing situation. Otherwise, Stone would have to drive the boys back and forth to school.

Jack was in summer school and only had two more days to complete, which he would do when they returned home or into a hotel the following week.

She heard the sound of a horse's hooves and glanced up. A pretty young girl with long, brown braids hanging over her shoulders appeared on the opposite side of the fence.

Stone introduced them to Melissa, Rachel Williams' daughter. Gina smiled when she noticed Jack's avid interest. The two of them, once they'd asked permission, moved away on their horses, each on their side of the fence, talking quietly.

Gina looked away from the young people, thankful for the sunglasses guarding her eyes against the sun setting in the west. She noted Stone wasn't wearing them, likely because his Stetson took care of the job. She watched Chris hunker down with Stone as they checked the fence. How companionable they seemed together, she mused, yet they'd just met. But then, her youngest son was a charmer, no doubt about it, and easy to get along with.

Her gaze swept across the fields at cows munching grass as she ambled along the fence line. Suddenly, she heard a rustling noise, then sizzling and came to an abrupt halt. Her heart pounded in her chest as she stared down at the ground.

Directly in her path, a sidewinder as thick as her fist lay coiled on the ground. Chills crept up her spine when it noticed her.

Drops of sweat dripped from her forehead and ran down her cheeks as it slithered toward her. Eventually, she managed to find her voice and she whispered as the creature drew closer, "Stone —help."

Praying he'd heard her words she suddenly felt the ground

rumbling beneath her feet. She looked up and saw a herd of cattle running parallel to the fence some distance away.

"Hey, Mom would you look at that!" Chris shouted.

Not only Gina heard, but the rattler, too. He halted his side-winding motion, lifted his head, stretching his neck about a foot off the ground. She glanced down at her insubstantial canvas tennis shoes and groaned inwardly, understanding now why Stone insisted the boys wear leather boots in the future, which he'd purchase for them he promised.

Gina felt tears sliding down her cheeks and sweat on her forehead as she stared down at the rattler. The snake started rattling its tail. She couldn't help moving, knew she shouldn't but she stumbled back a step then shrieked when an explosion rent the air.

She stared down at her feet, dumbfounded when she noticed the snake hadn't struck her as she'd expected. It was stretched out flat on the ground, unmoving, a hole in its side. Staying away from the fence itself, she held onto a post for dear life, trying to catch the breath she'd been holding.

Stone strode to Gina's side, Chris running alongside him. Gina groaned when she caught the panicked look on his face. Just then Jack and Melissa came trotting back. Chris's face was white as he looked down at the dead snake.

Gina felt strong arms surround her and she turned into Stone's welcoming embrace.

"It's all right," he whispered against her hair. "It's dead."

Shuddering, she wound her arms around his waist, realizing he'd likely just saved her life. After a short while she stepped back and tilted up her chin to meet his eyes. Then she reached up and gently touched the side of his face, surprised by the softness of his beard.

"You don't know how happy I am you brought that gun along."

Chris whispered, "Mom, you okay?"

She reached out a hand and drew him against her side. "Thanks to our tough rancher here, I'm fine."

Stone grinned. "Let's get out of here."

She nodded and they walked to his horse, hand in hand.

If Gina had seen the angry, confused expression on Jack's face, and Chris's happy one, she would have immediately dropped Stone's hand.

CHAPTER SEVEN

For the next several days, Chris and Jack rode out with Stone each day, working on fixing the fencing and doing other chores.

On Monday, Gina and her boys left Falcon's Ridge. Luckily, several non-smoking rooms had opened up at a Comfort Inn.

The boys had grumbled about leaving the ranch, but Gina pacified them when she told them they'd visit Stone the following weekend, when she would continue working with him to fulfill their contract, which included giving him dance lessons.

Gina's schedule was booked solid from Monday through Wednesday. On Thursday morning, as she opened her office door, she looked forward to a relatively quiet day to catch up on her paperwork. Just as she reached her desk the phone rang, and she snatched it up. "Smooth Edges Consultations."

Her brow furrowed when she heard a woman's cool voice ask for her.

"This is Gina Liberatti."

"Janet Miller, Mrs. Liberatti. The Principal from North High."

As soon as Principal Miller spoke, Gina recognized her voice and she stilled. She'd had first-hand experience with it on two other recent occasions. Gina breathed slowly in and out and squeezed the phone tight against her ear. "Is something wrong?"

"Unfortunately, yes. I was forced to suspend Jack from school for the rest of the session and he won't get any of the credit, either."

Darn, Jack, she mused, and this the final week. Now he wouldn't make up that lost credit in social studies he'd failed during the school year.

"What did he do?" Gina said, her voice trembling.

"He tried buying marijuana from another classmate, on school property. Our liaison police officer caught him."

"Oh, no," Gina groaned.

"We found the boys in the locker room showers after P.E. class. When they didn't show up for their next scheduled classes their absence was reported to the attendance office. I'm sorry, but you'll have to come and get him. I was forced to call the police."

"What do we have to do?"

"You need to speak with the authorities and decide upon a plan of action that will help your son."

"I understand. I'll be by to pick him up shortly."

Her hand shook as she hung up, her mind racing at the possibility that the legal system could very well take her son away from her and place him in foster care if she didn't get him straightened out.

A low, soft voice from somewhere in the vicinity of the doorway said, "What's going on, Gina?"

Gina's head shot up and she met Stone's piercing eyes as he stood in the doorway. She came to her feet and wrung her hands, wondering how much he'd overheard, trying to recall what she'd said.

"Oh, business as usual." She plastered an artificial smile on her lips as she came around her desk and met him in the middle of her office. "What brings you to town?"

He held up her purse. "You forgot something. This was the soonest I could get it here."

"I changed purses at your place and left that one behind I guess when I packed up. Thanks for coming all this way to return it, though."

He gave her the purse and that engaging smile of his. "You're welcome. Now, who was on the phone?"

Gina fidgeted and bit her lip as his eyes bored into hers.

"Was it one of the boys?"

She set her purse on the desk and then moved to the windows, wondering at the accuracy of his guess. As she watched the morning traffic her eyes filled with tears. Lord, how she wanted to confide in him.

"I—I'd rather not say."

"Try me," he said. "Might help you feel better."

Gina felt him come up behind her, surround her, turned her to face him. He held her hand and said, "Tell me what's going on. I'll help you if I can."

"Thanks for the offer, Stone, but I'll manage." She pulled her hand from his.

"You've got to talk to someone, Gina. I can see you're upset."

She was upset but the only one she could talk to and would was Jack. "I will."

"When?"

She frowned. "Would you please just let it go?"

His gentle grin turned devilish. "I've all the time in the world, darlin'." He sat down on her sofa, stretched his arms across the back and settled in.

He appeared big and tough, and he took up lots of space. Her spacious office suddenly seemed too small for the both of them.

She marched across the office to the door and opened it. He stayed put, one eyebrow arched as he waited.

She sighed and threw up her hands. "We'll talk later."

"Today?" he asked as he rose.

"When I come out to the ranch on Saturday."

He stopped beside her. "You're bringing the boys along, right?"

"Of course. Why?"

"I've a surprise for them. Instead of coming late afternoon come earlier, for lunch. We'll have tacos."

"After their ball games we'll come."

"Believe me when I say all I want to do is help."

She gulped and nodded, so tempted to tell him everything, but Jack was her problem. And she was working on it. She'd be attending her first Tough Love meeting tonight. Hopefully, the folks there would have suggestions for her that would make a difference.

He left then, closing the door behind him.

———

Later that evening, Mrs. Murphy watched the boys while Gina attended a tough love meeting.

She glanced down at her watch and saw she would be late if she didn't hurry. She pulled into the church parking lot and rushed from her car. Once inside the church she followed the hum of voices. At the far end of the hallway she stopped and stared into a room filled with tables set in a box-shape. Several chairs around the table were already occupied.

A feeling of apprehension and insecurity stopped her from moving inside the room and facing these strangers with her problems. After a moment she decided she had no choice since she'd reached the end of her own resourcefulness. Jack was in trouble which meant her family was, also. She needed to do this for him—for all of them.

A tall, athletically built woman with pretty blue eyes gave Gina a warm smile, revealing gleaming white toothpaste ad teeth. "Just sign in and make yourself a name tag."

Gina nodded and bent to her task. Soon after she sat down the woman started speaking.

"Welcome, everyone. For those who don't know me, I'm Natalie Grayson, one of the facilitators of San Antonio's Tough Love organization. To start out our meeting I'd like the new folks in the room to introduce themselves."

Gina and just one other woman were the only new people in the crowd. After they gave their names, Natalie continued with the meeting.

"Before we actually get into the sharing time of our meeting, we have a special guest with us this evening. Detective Connor Wayne with the San Antonio police department, is here to speak to us about Texas laws with regards to minors. Let's welcome him, shall we?"

Polite applause broke out as a tall, handsome blond-haired man sauntered to the front of the room. He stopped beside Natalie and stuck out his hand. "It's a pleasure to be here. Thanks for asking me to speak."

Something about his walk and the confidence he exuded reminded Gina of Stone. Her lips tilted up into a wide grin when Ms. Grayson's face turned pink and she stuttered her own thanks. Gina turned her gaze back to the man and decided he'd probably broken plenty of women's hearts in his lifetime.

He wore a black string tie, white shirt, blue jeans and a black suit jacket with western boots and belt. He was handsome and charming, and his manner very polished and professional. He was big and strong, what Gina would call a real 'heart throb'. The man stood before the group, hands clasped behind his back, stance wide. His appearance was a blend of professional law enforcer mixed with cowboy.

Gina looked around and saw the avid expressions on the other women's faces; looks that shouted, 'you can apprehend me any day of the week, you hunk!' She also caught the interested looks on the men's faces as they settled in to listen for any shred of advice to help with their family problems.

"I'm here today to tell you things you might want to hear, and some things you might not. The downside is that you're all here because you need help. The upside of it is I think I can make a difference."

At the end of the meeting Gina felt she'd been given effective tools to help correct Jack's behavior. The first step; if he didn't agree to sign a contract promising good behavior, she'd move on to step two. She'd always had her own set of household rules but had never thought to actually write them down and have Jack sign and agree to obey them. Anything was worth a shot at this point.

CHAPTER EIGHT

On Saturday afternoon, as Gina turned into the long driveway and passed beneath the horseshoe gateway leading to Falcon's Ridge Ranch, she thought about the minor success she'd accomplished in her household in the past two days. She knew it was too early to be so optimistic, but in her mind, she'd straddled a huge hurdle.

Jack had signed the contract she'd typed up, after arguing a bit about what he called an unreasonably early curfew, but she'd held firm to her convictions. He was grounded so she didn't have to worry about him going out with friends and not coming home on time.

She smiled as she parked her car alongside Stone's Bronco. The rules she'd learned from the tough love meeting were working, albeit not without argument from Jack. She applied a few rules to Chris as well in an effort not to be seen favoring one over the other. Each passing day was another baby step closer to having a well-functioning family life for her and her sons as she admitted to herself that things were running more smoothly at home.

She stayed in the car readying herself for the confrontation with Stone. There was no question in Gina's mind the blasted man possessed the ability to make her spill her guts, so she braced herself. She truly didn't want to tell him—didn't want to involve him too much in her life. Now that she'd finally gained some independence, she wasn't giving it up for any man, no matter how tempting he was. Especially a man like Stone, who exuded confidence and likely felt it was his God-given right to control every little thing around him.

Gina had been surprised this morning when Stone had arrived at her house. She'd had tons of errands to run, an appointment with her hairdresser for a trim, and a meeting with a client which she would cancel if she couldn't juggle it all. Stone had said he'd come to town to buy some tools, and that he'd take the boys back to the ranch with him for the day, after baseball practice ended, if she didn't mind.

Jack and Chris had both whooped and hollered until she'd given in. And they were ecstatic he would watch them play ball, even if it meant him spending half the time on one ball field watching one boy and then the other half on another field. Which she did all the time.

They hated tagging along with her when she had dozens of errands to run. But she also didn't like the fact Stone hadn't called first and told him as much. She bristled when she thought about the toothy smile he'd given her and promised he would next time.

Now she left the car, straightened her seersucker-striped narrow skirt, and tucked in the back of her white blouse. Reaching into the back seat, she hauled out her overnight bag where she'd packed a t-shirt, jeans, and loafers. She couldn't wait to change out of her business clothes. She slung her purse over her shoulder just as Marguerite appeared in the doorway.

"Hi, Marguerite." Gina forced a smile on her lips as she climbed the steps.

"You look exhausted," Marguerite fussed as she took Gina's jacket and hung it in the closet.

She sat down at the table, sipped the cup of coffee Marguerite set in front of her and thought, *so much for not working on Saturdays*. Ruby had inadvertently looked at the wrong calendar page when she'd booked Mrs. Vanderpool's next appointment, which ended up being today, a Saturday.

The house was peaceful—too peaceful. "Where is everybody?"

"Washing up. They should be down to eat soon, but be prepared," she warned.

Gina frowned. "For what?"

"Stoney put your boys to work today. Their scrawny butts were dragging when they came in twenty minutes ago. I wouldn't be surprised if they turned in early."

"Are they all right?" Gina asked worriedly. "Maybe I should just take them home."

"They're fine. Stoney wouldn't hurt them."

Jack and Chris chose that moment to trudge into the kitchen, their hair wet from showering. Then she noticed their hang dog expressions.

"Are you guys okay?"

Their sagging, nodding heads were no reassurance. She came to her feet, moved to the cupboard, and pulled down four plates.

Marguerite took the plates from her and scolded, "You sit and drink your coffee."

"Helping you is the least I can do. If I were at home, I'd have to cook dinner and clean up by myself. This is a treat."

Marguerite grumbled, "All right, if you insist." She transferred refried beans from a pot on the stove to a bowl and placed it in the center of the table.

"I'm going to change into my jeans," Gina said. "I'll be right back."

The older woman looked her over. "You look fine the way you are. Stoney likes skirts on ladies."

At that moment, Stone strode into the kitchen. "Now, Marguerite, you're making me sound sexist." He gave Gina a smile and she noted the twinkling humor in his eyes as they slid down her body from head to toe, then back up. "I enjoy a woman's shape in a pair of decent-fitting jeans, too."

Marguerite just shook her head as she headed for the back door. "Well, goodnight, you two."

"Thanks, Marguerite," Stone called after her.

Gina met Stone's eyes, gentle, yet hard—a bit uncompromising. While his beard had dried from his shower, his dark hair was still wet. His chambray shirt and blue jeans seemed to accentuate his strong body. He took his seat at the head of the table. Gina finished setting it and left the kitchen to change clothes.

The supper hour was uncharacteristically quiet. Jack and Chris were too tired to utter so much as a single word. Once they finished eating, they immediately asked to be excused.

Stone said, "Good idea, boys. I'll be waking you up around five-thirty."

They didn't say a word but groaned as they moved to Gina's side, surprising her when they leaned down, pecked her cheek, and said goodnight. Jack yelped when she squeezed his hand.

"Jack? What's wrong?"

"Nothing."

She heard the sullen tone in his voice, and she held onto his hand. She turned it palm up and stared in horror at two nickel-sized blisters. "What happened to your hands?"

"I said nothing!" He jerked his hand free and followed Chris out of the kitchen.

Gina turned to Stone and found his back to her as he stood at the counter pouring a cup of coffee. Eyeing his taut, trim backside, she asked, "What kind of work was Jack doing today?"

"Typical stuff that needs to be done around a ranch—mending fences, for example." He turned around, cup in hand and leaned back against the counter.

Gina rose and moved to Stone's side. As she refilled her own cup she said, "Did you see his hands?"

"He's developed some bad blisters. Once they heal up, they'll turn into some mighty fine calluses."

She scowled. "He can't work until they're completely healed."

"Sure he can. The blisters will be a daily reminder for him to wear his gloves in the future. I've already disinfected them and gave him some antibiotic ointment cream. He'll be fine."

She watched him swallow down his mug of coffee. "You mean to tell me you are punishing him for forgetting to wear gloves?" she asked incredulously.

"He didn't forget. He chose to ignore my direction to wear them. Chris hasn't a single blister because he followed orders."

Gina carried her cup back to the table and sank into her chair. "Jack is not mending any more fences until his hands have healed."

Stone leveled a hard look on her. "It won't kill him to be up and on his horse by six a.m." He set down his cup and reached for the coffeepot once more.

"Tomorrow is Sunday and he'll be sleeping in his own bed and attending church in the morning."

"What time is church?"

"Eleven."

Stone nodded. "Fine. I'll put him on light duty. He'll have plenty of time to do chores before church. By the way, did I tell you the boys want to spend the night?"

"What they want and what they'll get are two different things. We're leaving for home soon," she warned.

Stone sat down and stretched out his legs. "We've got to finish building that section of fence before the new herd arrives day after tomorrow."

"Isn't that what you pay your hands to do?"

"I'm short on hands at the moment. Besides, Jack and Chris begged me to allow them to work, I didn't force them."

"They did?" Whenever she mentioned 'housework' her boys griped and groaned. But then she decided if she were a young boy, she'd rather work outside pounding nails than do housework, too.

"Absolutely. I'm paying them rookie hand wages."

"I knew there had to be a reason why they were doing all that work for you and figured money might have something to do with it." She gave him a crooked smile. "You wore them out."

He grinned, his even white teeth flashing. "Sure did, didn't I?" He set his empty cup down, moved around the table to her side where he took her hand. "By the way, don't think I've forgotten about that phone call the other morning."

Gina heard the steely tone in his voice as he pulled her to her feet and led her from the kitchen.

She tried putting him off. "It's a long drive home. If I leave now, we'll get there before dark, and—"

"You're not leaving. You'll be spending the night, same as the boys. Besides, I saw you packed a suitcase—a good thing. Obviously, we're on the same wavelength."

She opened her mouth to dispute it when he inserted, "I know we are so don't deny it."

"Excuse me?" she said indignantly, pulling her arm from his grasp.

"I'll bet money they're already asleep." He took her hand again and tugged her down the hallway. "You don't want to wake them up now, do you?"

Gina sighed, hating her weakness for this guy. And he also made a lot of sense, besides. It was too late to drive home now.

"No," she replied, "You're right."

"What was that?" he asked, his hand cupping an ear.

"Smart aleck," she groused.

He just grinned, released her as they entered the family room and closed the door behind them. Moving to the bar, he asked, "Would you like a drink?"

"Nothing for me." She positioned herself behind the sofa and watched him mix himself a scotch and water.

"I can't force you to tell me," he said when he finished.

He moved closer to Gina drink in hand, a devastating grin on his lips.

She closed her eyes to blot him out, the little voice inside telling her, *be strong!*

"Believe me when I say I want to help you, Gina."

"I'm dealing with it," she tightly replied.

"Sit...relax." He sank down on the sofa, tilted his head back and took a healthy swallow of scotch.

Warily, Gina watched him then sighed and sank down on the opposite end of the sofa.

"I heard how you're dealing with it." He was staring down at his drink and he raised his gaze to her and added, "I didn't like it."

"It's not your concern."

"I'll find out sooner or later."

Her eyes widened. "How?"

"I've ways."

His confidence annoyed her, yet as she gazed into his gentle, caring face she decided to confess the truth. A big strong shoulder to cry on might be helpful. "I'm having trouble with Jack."

Once she began telling him about the call from the principal she couldn't stop. When she finished, she felt as though the weight of her problems were being lifted from her shoulders. Even if there wasn't anything Stone could do to help, it felt wonderful having someone to confide in. It was tough being a single parent and these were the times she missed her husband the most.

She rose, paced from one end of the den to the other. "I'm disgusted with myself because I just don't seem to have control over him. He's become surly over the past year since his father's death. He outright tells me 'no' when I ask him to help with chores. He stays out late with friends and never obeys the curfew I set for him."

"How many times has Jack been suspended from school in the past?"

Gina sighed. "Once last year and twice this year." She bit her lip as she met his frowning, concerned expression. "I'm afraid it's getting to be a habit with him. And this was summer school," she groaned.

"I hate asking this, Gina, but do you know if he's a user?"

She frowned. "What are you talking about?"

"Do you think there's a possibility he uses drugs?"

Gina halted directly in front of him and sputtered, "He doesn't! I know that in the past he's experimented a few times with his friends, but I don't believe he's a steady user. What makes you think he is?"

Stone narrowed his eyes and came to his feet. "A certain amount of rebellion is typical for teens but not the explosive anger and uncooperative behavior you mentioned, and that I've witnessed firsthand. Let me explain something; kids start out using the soft stuff. It's easy to purchase and cheaper, but when it becomes tame and unexciting, some kids move on to hard drugs. I'd sure hate to see Jack screw up his life and land in jail or kill himself."

"What can I do?" She shivered at the possibility of her oldest son being hooked on drugs.

"If you believe he's on something cut him off any supply of money first. Talk to other parents of the kids he hangs with and see if they're experiencing the same behavior with their children. Have you had him tested for the stuff?"

She shook her head.

"Has he seen a psychiatrist? Or a counselor since his father died?"

"For several months he did. Right after his father's death but not recently. We stopped the appointments because, to both the counselor and I, it seemed he'd accepted Charlie's death."

"I think it's time you got a second opinion. You're solid as a rock, and Chris seems to be doing okay, but Jack isn't," Stone said flatly. "I can tell by how he doesn't trust me around you. He's still hurting, feeling sorry for himself because his dad's left him."

"But why would he be so suspicious about you?" she asked as she sat down.

Stone took his seat beside her again. "Because he's scared someone like me will take his mom away from him. Bear in mind, he's already lost one parent."

"I hadn't even thought about that."

Stone shifted his weight on the sofa and moved closer. Gina slipped toward him, struggled to right herself and muttered, "Sorry."

His arm clamped around her shoulders and he held her in place at his side. She looked up and found a half-smile on his lips, kindness in his eyes. His gentle look warmed her from the inside out and took her breath away. She relaxed against him, deciding there was no sense in fighting her attraction to him. He was just too damned tempting—too irresistible.

"I'd like to make a suggestion."

She nodded, waiting for him to continue, utterly conscious of his big warm body so close to hers.

"First thing Monday morning, you've got to make some appointments for him."

Gina frowned and pulled back from him. "What sort of appointments?"

"To see a different counselor and to be drug-tested."

"I'll think about it."

When he scowled, she held up one palm and said, "Now hold on a minute. Jack's my son and I've already taken a step in the right direction. I attended a Tough Love meeting Thursday night. You've probably never heard of this parent support group before, but they were fantastic. They gave me all sorts of information and—"

"I know the group well," Stone interrupted. "Connor Wayne spoke, didn't he?"

She gave him a wide-eyed look. "Now how would you know that?"

"I used to be a in law enforcement and on the force with him until five years ago when I retired and inherited this ranch from my uncle. He works out of one of the stations in town." He leaned close and smiled into her eyes. "You are taking the right step with Jack, using Tough Love as a resource, but getting him into the professionals for drug testing and counseling is the next important step."

She didn't reply but closed her eyes, shutting him out. It seemed the only people she knew who sought that sort of help were dysfunctional families. Hers wasn't, or was it? Her eyes snapped open when he pressed closer, invading her space.

Gina narrowed her eyes and said, "If you think that little move will make me give you the answer you're demanding, you're dead wrong, cowboy. I plan on thinking about your suggestion for a few days before I decide to call upon outside intervention again."

He reached out and tucked one strand of hair behind her ear. She held her breath when he leaned close and planted a small, whispery kiss on that exposed earlobe. Then he moved back and met her eyes with a smile.

Softly, he drawled, "You've got to trust me on this, Gina. In the past, I've worked with kids like Jack. Don't you see how important it is that you get him help?"

She couldn't tell him more than she'd already confessed. It wasn't easy raising two sons on one income, and Charlie had left her very little money. She'd taken that small amount and had invested it into college funds for the boys, which she refused to touch.

Because she was in business for herself, she carried her own health coverage. She hadn't picked up the mental health clause protection because she hadn't felt she needed it and it was expensive. Apparently, she would have to now, especially if he needed drug counseling. She sighed. Just when she thought she was getting ahead something happened.

"I want to help him," she choked out, "but I don't have insurance to cover that area."

"I'd hand you the money in a heartbeat to pay for a counselor but know damned well you wouldn't accept it," he scolded. "But there are agencies that help people who don't have insurance or can't pay. You may qualify for that help. Call the county and check it out. You owe it to Jack."

She looked down at her clenched hands. "I will. First thing Monday."

"Good girl." He smiled, rose, and took her hands in his, pulling her to her feet. "It's getting late and I haven't had my dance lesson yet."

She fondly recalled their first lesson and she couldn't help grinning.

"Now, why is my learning to dance funny?" he asked.

She'd heard the hesitant, slightly belligerent tone in his voice and explained, "It's not. It's just that, well, you caught me off guard when we danced together that first time in my office." She looked at him long and steady. "You knew how to dance all along, didn't you?"

He shrugged. "I've picked up a few things along the way, but you know something?"

"What?"

With a huge grin he moved to the stereo and pushed a button until he found a mellow tune. He returned to her side and took her in his arms. "It doesn't matter anymore."

"Why not?"

"Because I don't have to worry about impressing Rachel. I've decided she isn't the right woman for me."

Gina's brow shot up. "What about marrying by Christmas? You've no one else in mind, have you?"

"As a matter of fact, I may." He started moving her to the music. "Time will tell."

CHAPTER NINE

As they danced in his library, Stone thought they did well together. It took all of his willpower to keep his hands in a dance position and not wander all over her sweet curves. But he was surprised when she didn't protest as he drew her fully against him.

This Saturday evening was different. She'd let her guard down, including confessing her greatest fears to him about Jack. It was good that she was learning to trust him.

Sure, he'd thought Rachel was the woman he'd wanted to marry, but Gina had changed his mind. Even though he'd only known her a very short while, there was something growing between them. He was pragmatic enough to know it couldn't be love—yet. But he didn't discount the possibility of their relationship growing and changing. Rachel's spread no longer attracted him. He'd just have to dig himself a new well.

Doubts entered his mind, then. Everything about Gina was desirable, but was he ready to be a father to two boys, one who desperately wanted a dad, the other who didn't and was currently going through turbulent teen years? But Stone wanted Gina in his life, in what way, shape or form, he was still uncertain. Once he got to know her better, he'd know, but she wasn't making it easy.

She liked him well enough, he knew, but she was being careful around him. He'd already guessed, from the little she'd told him about her father and her late husband, becoming involved with a controlling man was out of the question.

Admitting he was of like disposition and attitude as the past men in her life didn't bother him a bit; it was the truth. But he knew it would matter to Gina. It was damned hard taming his natural inclinations. Often, he found himself biting his tongue, especially with regards to her boys. Why she allowed them so much freedom of choice was beyond him—from their choice of clothing to Jack's shoulder-length hair.

He grinned when he thought how he'd gently taunted him about looking like a girl. Jack had taken it in stride, shrugging him off, while Gina had come to his defense like a lioness protecting her cub.

Stone frowned as he recalled her saying something about Jack's freedom of expression. He kept his opinions to himself because he wanted all the cards to fall in his favor when and if he decided she was the one for him, and in one short week, he'd come to realize he was more than halfway on his way to that conclusion.

As they danced her legs bumped his and her pelvis gently, provocatively, rubbed against his body with each step.

The music ended and they paused. Gina stepped back and stared into his eyes. He lowered his head, his gaze on her lips until he couldn't refuse their sweet invitation.

His kiss started out gently, but soon his lips seared hers with a passion that threatened to consume them. The taste of her was sweet intoxication. He slid a hand over her hip until he reached her buttocks, cupped her, and pulled her firmly against his pelvis. His other hand stretched down between them, to her front, pausing at the apex of her thighs.

He groaned and stroked her with the entire palm of his hand

through her jeans. Though the fabric was thick he felt her heated warmth.

"Why aren't you wearing that little dress you wore the first time we danced, without stockings?" he whispered in her ear. He rubbed his hand hard against the seam of her jeans, up and down the inside of her thighs.

"What?" She tipped her head back and her drowsy, sexy expression spoke volumes. Stone was ready to tear every article of clothing from her body.

Snatching her up in his arms he carried her to his desk and set her down. Then he coerced her legs apart and stepped between them. Leaning down he kissed her with a fierceness he wouldn't have been able to gentle if he'd tried. His breathing stilled at the same moment his heart began pounding heavily when her fingers moved to his belt buckle and paused.

"Don't stop now, lady," he drawled, nuzzling her earlobe.

Gina tipped her head back and met his eyes. "You knew I was attracted to you from the beginning, didn't you?"

He shrugged. "I guessed maybe you were."

"Ah, so modest." She sighed. "You've been with many women, haven't you?"

"Not as many as you might think. I've been very, very discriminate. I'm safe if that's what you're asking."

"Well, I wouldn't say that *safe* is the precise word I'd use to describe you, but I'm glad you've been cautious."

Her next words amazed him, humbled him, and made him even more eager for her than he already was.

"You know, Stone, other than my husband, I've never been with another man."

Knowing he was only the second man in her life made him feel ten feet tall. Her eyes took on a glazed look and his heart soared when he saw the ardent look on her face. She wanted him.

"It's been a long time since I've been with a man."

Stone swallowed. "I'd guessed as much. I want you, Gina, more than I ever imagined I'd want a woman."

"Ditto."

He tilted her chin up with a shaky fist. "Is that a fact?"

"Yes, I've been denying it but I have to be truthful about this." She smiled and he gave her a suspicious look.

"Tell me you want me as much as I want you."

She blushed. "I thought I just did."

"Nope. Ditto doesn't count. Not by a long shot."

The gentle look in her eyes and the curve of her pretty lips nearly did him in. "Oh, I want you all right. Even though I know this is temporary, we can still have this time together, can't we?"

"Oh, yeah," he breathed, too aroused to contradict her words, knowing he wanted much more time than a few minutes—a few times together. They were meant to be together. He'd tell her later.

She tilted back her head and he found her lips again.

The clock ticking in the corner of the room was the only sound to be heard, other than the erratic breathing of a man and a woman discovering each other's secrets. Stone finally lifted his head and stroked her hair off her forehead.

"Have you any idea what you're doing to me?" Gina whispered.

Stone just grinned. He placed his hands on her hips and deftly unsnapped her jeans. Then he smiled at her surprised gasp when he delved one hand down the front. Leaning toward her he kissed her again. When he raised his head this time, ready to suggest they move to her room or his, or hell, even the sofa, he stilled and stared into the mirror above the fireplace. *Damn!*

Stone caught Jack's furious expression for a split second as he passed the library. Stone closed his eyes, felt his stomach lurch. Damn! He'd forgotten about the open door. His mind raced as he wondered what a fifteen-year-old boy knew about men and women. Jack had likely had some sex education in school and, possibly, some experience with girls. Although to Stone's mind fifteen was on the young side for a sexual relationship. Or was it?

He tried recalling what he'd known about girls when he was Jack's age and cringed. He'd known a hell of a lot, but then, he'd grown up in the fast lane, on the seedier side of the tracks.

Smiling down at Gina's aroused expression as he held her in his arms, he released her, reached down and snapped her jeans.

He sighed at the stunned look in her eyes, but said in a light, calm tone, "Next time, lady, we'll finish this, and it'll be in my bed, or yours."

She arched one eyebrow. "Promises, promises. What makes you think there'll be a next time, cowboy? By the way, was there a reason we stopped?"

Stone stared at her—saw the disappointment in her face and his heart gladdened. Now he had to make her understand it wasn't anything she'd done or said that had prompted him to stop making love to her.

He searched to find the right words. After a moment, he said, "I want us both to be absolutely sure before we delve any further into a relationship."

Then he swept her up in his arms and kissed her soundly. He strode out of the library and, once he reached her bedroom door, he set her down. Stone leaned forward and smacked his hands against the solid oak, effectively trapping her.

Tracing his lips across her forehead and chin, he finally settled them on her lips. When he ended the kiss, he lifted his head and smiled into her eyes. She gasped when he worked his hand beneath her shirt until he found the front closure of her bra and released it.

She laughed and batted at his hands, glancing around self-consciously. "Enough!" She frowned and added, "You know, I thought I heard footsteps earlier, but I must have imagined it."

"Must have," he agreed. He tucked a fist under her chin and kissed her.

With his eyes focused on her he opened the door. "Good night, darlin'." Gently, he shoved her inside. Suddenly, the door swung open again. "Lock the door."

Gina looked at him, confused. "Why?"

"'Cause I won't be responsible for my actions if I find it unlocked before morning."

As Stone strode away, moved toward the west wing of the house, he was glad he'd decided to install the boys in the guestrooms some distance away.

Stone didn't look forward to confronting Jack but knew he had to clear things up between them now, before the kid had too much time to stew.

CHAPTER TEN

J ack stormed into his bedroom and threw himself on the bed. He hated his mother and Stone. How could she do something like that? It would be different if they were engaged or something, but they meant nothing to each other. Suddenly, unwanted memories of the past school year entered his mind, particularly thoughts of one of his classmates, Jenny Piccolo.

He and Jenny had sat together, shoulder to shoulder, at a tall lab table in the very last row in science class. A long, canvas apron ran the perimeter of the table and hung down low, brushing their knees. She'd startled him the first time she'd touched his thigh and had moved it higher until she'd reached her destination.

He'd immediately started sweating, shocked and embarrassed at first. After that he'd grown enthralled with Jenny and her talented hands that managed to send him skyrocketing. Jenny had been sixteen, two years older than Jack, even though they were in the same class. But Jenny had failed a grade and being an older, knowledgeable woman, she'd fascinated him.

And she had a car. The first time she'd offered him a ride home from school he'd jumped at the chance since he hated the over-crowded, long bus ride home. Within a short while he noticed they were traveling in the opposite direction from his house. When he mentioned it, she said she thought they could stop and have a soda and get to know each other at her house. He thought about her hands on him under the lab counter and didn't object.

It turned out both of her parents worked, and she was an only child. Jack's last two months of ninth grade he'd passed in hot, lusty sex with Jenny, until one day she told him she was pregnant and wouldn't be returning to school the following year.

He'd panicked at first and then informed her he'd do the right thing by getting a job and helping her out until they were old enough to marry.

She'd laughed and had dropped him like a hot potato.

Andy Paulson, a guy who'd graduated last year, was the father and had owned up to it, she said. When Jack told her *he* could very well be the father, she'd said it wasn't possible. She'd been pregnant for a month before she'd been assigned to sitting beside him in science class. She further explained she'd only indulged in a fling with him to make Andy jealous.

Jack had learned a lot about women during that month, and it was unfortunate that it was more than a little likely, in the years to come, that his memories of his first love would be tainted.

To his way of thinking, Jenny had been a tramp and he fought his feelings that his mother may be one as well. His father had been dead only a year and she had no business wanting another man in her life so soon.

No man could ever replace his father.

———

In his own bedroom, Stone quickly undressed and showered in the adjoining bathroom. Thoughts of Gina taking a shower with him made him smile. He'd thoroughly enjoy scrubbing her skin until it turned pretty pink. Then he grimaced as he stepped out, shaking his head, and staring down in disgust at his burgeoning arousal. The mere thought of her was driving him insane.

He donned a pair of clean briefs followed by basketball shorts and a t-shirt then braced himself for his confrontation with Jack. He made a left turn as he moved down a hallway leading to Jack's door.

A brief knock and the door immediately swung open. When Jack saw Stone, he slammed his hand against the door but wasn't quick enough. Stone stuck his foot into the small opening and shouldered open the door.

"Oldest trick in the book," Stone drawled.

Jack turned away without a word, moved to the window and stared out into the night. He stood huddled, his arms crossed, shoulders hunched.

"You saw us, didn't you?"

Jack didn't reply.

"You saw us kissing in the library," Stone insisted. "We stopped before—"

Jack whirled around, his face pain-racked, his hands clenched into fists at his sides. He took a step, made a jerky move toward Stone then stopped, his face twisted in fury.

"Go ahead, son," Stone said softly. "Get it out of your system."

"How many times do I have to tell you, man? I'm not your goddamned son!"

"I know," Stone said soothingly, "I understand that you miss your father, but—"

Before Stone could finish, a flying fist smacked his jaw. He managed to stay on his feet when Jack hurled himself at him, swinging wildly. Stone held up his arms, fending off the blows, but didn't strike back, knowing he could floor the boy if he did.

He had to admit Jack was stronger than he appeared. Dull, thudding blows struck Stone's forearms as he kept them up until Jack tired and slowed down.

Stone made his move then and hauled the boy to the bed, threw him face down and jammed his knee in his back.

Jack struggled to get away. "Let me up!"

Pressing down, Stone flattened Jack on the bed. "Quiet!" he hissed, "You don't want to wake your mom and Chris, or do you? This situation might be real tough to explain."

Jack ceased his struggles. "Get off me you pervert!"

"Where in the hell did you learn that crap?" Stone snarled. "You going to be sensible and shut up and listen?"

"You can't take his place!" Jack sobbed. And then, more softly, "No one can."

Stone's heart clenched. "If you mean your dad, I agree. I know what you're feeling, but I got to be up front with you and tell you, I like your mom a lot."

"Let me up. Please," Jack grudgingly replied.

Stone rose and sank down on the edge of the bed.

Jack scrambled to his feet. "You don't know what I feel."

Stone had yearned for a father all those years his mother had raised him alone, but she'd never allowed another man into her life.

"You're damned lucky you had your father with you for as long as you did," Stone replied. "I never knew mine."

"What do you mean? Everybody's got a dad." Jack was clearly puzzled by Stone's admission.

Stone shrugged. "Not me. My mama raised me by herself. My mama never married my dad."

"Did she...did she ever get married?"

"Nope. And I don't have any brothers or sisters, so you're lucky you got Chris."

"Do you love my mom, or do you just wanna stick it in her?"

Stone was astonished and somewhat embarrassed by the question. Lounging back against the headboard he stared at Jack and tried to decide how to answer him. Finally, he said, "Your mom's been real lonely. You know?"

"Some answer," Jack grumbled.

"I'll be truthful—"

"Sure you will," Jack retorted, his voice laced with sarcasm.

Stone narrowed his eyes and started again. "I have strong feelings for your mom. I don't know if I love her, but I want her, no doubt about it. I'm not even sure if I know what love means, and there is the fact I've only known her a very short while."

"I think she likes you a lot."

Stone knew he was right, even though Gina was being cautious. The expression on her face whenever she looked at him spoke volumes. The old saying, 'she wore her heart on her sleeve' appeared to have merit. The idea of Gina's attraction for him turning to love made him feel extraordinarily good, confounding him.

In the past, whenever a woman got too close for comfort he'd run in the opposite direction. But now, since he'd decided it was time he married, he wasn't running any more. Until he'd met Gina, he'd truly believed Rachel would be the perfect mate for him. He'd since learned that livestock, land, and wells weren't important when it came to finding the right woman. As a matter of fact, *things* didn't matter at all.

He patted the bed beside him. "Sit down, Jack. You'll be more comfortable."

Jack's shoulders slumped and he shook his head. Then he snatched up a straight-backed chair and sprawled in it, facing Stone.

"There's more wrong here besides my interest in your mother, isn't there?"

"I've got problems of my own," Jack said.

"You can tell me. You know you can."

Stone was surprised that he'd managed to find the right words to say when Jack proceeded to pour out his story about Jenny. When he was through, Stone found it hard to believe. Sex and a fifteen-year-old wasn't a good mix, especially if it had been a bad experience.

"I thought I loved her you know?" Jack said.

Stone saw Jack's face turn pink. He rose, crossed to Jack, and swung an arm around his shoulder. Looking seriously down at the boy's surprised face he said, "Women are something else, aren't they? They twist you into a million knots, and once they get you where they want, they do terrible things to us guys, don't they?"

Jack looked at Stone as a slow smile crossed his lips. Then they both burst into gut-wrenching laughter, choking in their efforts to be quiet.

"Bet you wouldn't have traded a minute of what happened between you and Jenny for anything. Am I right?" Stone said.

Jack wiggled his eyebrows in a very adult male fashion. "Not a minute. I'll remember her for the rest of my life, even if she was a tramp."

Stone's smile slipped. "Don't ever talk about a woman that way. Sometimes things happen that are beyond a woman's control. Jenny wasn't a tramp. She was looking for love. Perhaps she didn't get enough of it from her folks. Who knows? Maybe that's why she got pregnant—for the attention."

"Yeah, I guess," Jack replied, unconvinced.

"Get some sleep, pardner. There are chores to be done in the morning."

Jack groaned.

Stone returned to his room and crawled into bed, wondering what it would be like being married to Gina. Would she cater to him as she did her boys? He enjoyed Marguerite making his meals and cleaning up the kitchen, but he paid her to do the chores. It meant he could concentrate on running the ranch. But Marguerite's performing the household chores wasn't the same as a wife making supper for him.

He chuckled to himself, knowing well what most women today would think of his antiquated expectations in a wife. Hell, knowing how important Gina's work was to her, she'd likely tell him to hire himself a laundress and a maid in addition to a cook!

But then he thought of the many things he would willingly do for her as her husband, and decided it wasn't too unrealistic of him to expect some measure of domesticity in a wife.

———

Stone met Gina the following Wednesday evening at her office as planned. They walked about eight blocks until they reached the Paseo del Rio, the River Walk bordering the San Antonio River. Stone was starving so they stopped to eat supper at a Mexican Café. They sat at a table outside, under a broad gold and black striped umbrella, ate tacos and drank beer.

An hour later they entered a hair salon Gina knew was one of the best in San Antonio. The barber was a tall, delicate-appearing man with body-piercings that made Stone cringe. The barber gave Stone the once over, making him feel unduly uncomfortable before directing him to a chair.

Stone hesitantly took a seat. He stilled when the barber, who said his name was Timmy, secured a towel around his neck. Over the towel he draped a large rectangular-shaped piece of vinyl.

Gina laughed aloud when Timmy winked at Stone in the mirror and Stone's complexion turned an interesting shade of pink. Now she sat in the outer lobby away from the proceedings, on tenterhooks, waiting for the outcome of Stone's haircut and shave.

He'd warned her about the scar on his face, but she said it wouldn't detract from his looks, and Timmy was a master stylist in great demand. She was stunned however when a short half hour later Stone ambled into the lobby, a grinning Timmy at his side.

"I thought you were going to shave off his beard and mustache?" Gina said, noticing he still wore whiskers.

Stone rubbed his chin. "Look…Tim's a genius. He trimmed it up nice and short. And the haircut's outstanding."

Outstanding? Good grief, Gina mused. Timmy's speech had rubbed off on Stone.

She rose and walked over to Stone. Reaching up she touched his cheek and his chin and smiled at the marked improvement, then turned to Timmy. "You've done a wonderful job. Thanks so much."

"No prob, Gina, baby. Bring him back *any* time."

Timmy winked at Stone again. This time Stone only gave him a wry look before leaving.

Gina tucked her arm through Stone's as they walked down the sidewalk. "Is it that bad?" she asked softly.

He gazed down at her from his formidable height. "Is what bad?"

"The scar. You had psyched yourself into completely shaving off the beard, but apparently had second thoughts."

Stone pulled on his denim shirt collar and murmured, "Guess I did. It's not a pretty sight. Maybe for Halloween, I will."

"That's the most ridiculous thing I ever heard, Stone Mitchell! Did you think you'd scare me if you shaved it off?"

"No, but I'd scare myself." He sighed. "Suffice it to say this scar is a daily reminder of the life I'd led back when I thought I was saving mankind. I learned the hard way that most of all I did or said made little difference. I got the hell out while I still had a life."

"But—"

"I'd rather not talk about it now, if you don't mind," he said, hating the coolness in his tone. But he truly wasn't ready to discuss the near calls he'd had in his past career—how many times he'd nearly lost his life.

———

By mid-afternoon Gina was both physically and mentally exhausted. It had taken much coercion on her part to get Stone to part with his hard-earned money on new clothing. She'd managed to talk him into purchasing two pairs of serviceable blue jeans in a dressier, designer-brand. Gina found three shirts, a white long-sleeved dress shirt and two lightweight cotton ones for casual wear. The most daunting hurdle had been getting him fitted for a suit.

She'd dragged him in to Galman's Menswear where a pretty young blonde took her sweet time measuring him. Gina grew more irritated by the minute, especially when Stone appeared to be enjoying the woman's attention.

Gina hadn't meant to get prickly, but she'd grown thoroughly tired of the woman repeatedly touching and measuring Stone's shoulders and waist. She'd snapped at her and told her if she didn't have the measurements by now, perhaps she should call for her supervisor's assistance.

Thankfully, it didn't take Stone long to decide upon a basic black, no-frills suit, and Gina agreed. He'd appeared sinfully handsome, the black suit a wonderful foil to his dark complexion and hair.

After spending the entire day shopping and arguing with Stone about clothing choices, Gina was thankful the shopping trip had ended. Bone-tired weariness settled over her as she sat down in his car. It didn't help that she hadn't been sleeping well, wondering why Stone had stopped in midstream making love to her last Saturday.

And they'd missed church Sunday because she'd slept in due to her insomnia that night. This just wasn't good, and she made a note to talk to Stone about moving up their Saturday dance lesson time so that they had time to return home earlier.

Besides, her boys were starting to ask questions about them, especially Chris. He'd embarrassed her Sunday before leaving the ranch when he point-blank asked them when they were going to get hitched.

She'd stumbled over a reply and had turned an irritated look on Stone when he just sank back against her car and grinned, allowing her to do the honors of explaining. He should have backed up her answer that they weren't getting married and that theirs was a business relationship. Since his next-door neighbor wasn't a wife contender any longer, according to Stone, she still needed to smooth his edges for another woman. And that woman wasn't her, though she had to admit the man knew how to kiss, among other things. She guessed he could easily talk her out of her clothes in a heartbeat.

They arrived at the ranch with several shopping bags.

Stone grumbled, "Never have I bought so many clothes before."

"You'll be thankful you did when you begin courting," Gina said, her heart clenching at the thought.

She waited to hear Stone's negative reply, begged to hear him say she was the only woman he wanted to court, but he didn't. He just left the house, said he had chores to do. Her boys followed him outside.

Half an hour later, as she stood in front of the stove stirring a kettle of chili Marguerite had prepared for them earlier in the day, Stone and the boys tramped in the back door. She took in their glum faces. Stone looked pole-axed while Jack appeared belligerent.

She smiled tentatively. "You three look as though you've had fights with your best friends."

"Why'd you tell him, Mom?" Jack shouted, taking Gina by surprise.

"Go to your room," Stone snapped. "Once you've cooled off, we can sit down and discuss this problem, and our options."

Stone swore under his breath then raked his hand through his hair as he watched Jack stalk down the hallway, Chris on his heels.

"What wasn't I supposed to tell you?" Gina said.

"That Jack had used drugs."

"Ah. I can see why that would upset him," she said slowly. "He admires you and doesn't want you to be disappointed and think badly of him."

"That's not why he's upset. I wouldn't have even brought it up if I hadn't caught him behind the barn lighting up. It wasn't a cigarette, Gina," he said. "He accused me of spying on him."

"Oh, no!" she groaned. "I'm sorry. I know you'd never do that."

"But I was," he said grimly. "Ever since you told me about the school suspensions, I've been keeping an eye on him. You've got to take this seriously. You've got to get him counseling and into some kind of drug rehabilitation, too."

"You mean put him in some place—lock him up?"

Stone nodded. "Temporarily, until he completes an addiction program."

"No! If he's locked up with kids that have the same problem, it'll only encourage him to keep on doing it when he's released."

"It may, but there's also a chance he'll stay clean. He needs help."

"I know he does. I'll call a psychologist next week and see if I can get him into counseling."

"Thought you were going to do that last week," Stone said. He sank into a chair at the table. "I know of several psychologists. I'll have a friend at the police station pull some phone numbers for you."

She nodded. "Thanks but no thanks. I am getting this under control."

"The boys hate living in a room in a hotel. Stay here at the ranch."

"We can't. I'm afraid my sons are becoming too attached to you. Besides, as of tomorrow, we can move back into our house." She gave him a sad smile. "Thanks for your help. I appreciate it."

Stone sat in silence as he watched Gina amble down the hallway, shoulders slumped. He cared for her and her boys and only wanted the best for them, which was how he imagined a man should feel about the woman he loves. *Whoa! Where in the hell had that come from?* He sighed, realizing the truth. He'd fallen in love with Gina.

Gina knew she was doing the right thing severing the ties to Stone. Her boys would be angry, but they were all growing too close to him, becoming dependent on him. She couldn't allow that to happen.

Ever since Charlie had died, she'd worked hard to start up her business. She'd accomplished her goal to become self-sufficient and successful, which meant she'd never have to count on a man again for support. She'd come a long way gaining confidence in herself and her abilities. Her mother had never worked a day outside the home since Gina's dominating Italian father hadn't allowed it. It had never seemed to bother her mother, but then, times had changed.

Gina had only herself to blame for losing out on the opportunity to attend college, and to go on to a career after high school because she'd gotten pregnant. Only after she'd married Charlie did she discover he was cut of the same cloth as her father. She'd never held a job until she started up her business.

Later, as she stood on Stone's back porch, her car packed and ready to leave, she saw him leave the barn and head straight for her. Jack slid by as he left the house, rudely bumped her in passing. She gasped, opened her mouth to chastise him but stopped when Stone met up with Jack at the foot of the steps.

"You owe your mom an apology."

Jack snarled, "Why?"

"You know why," Stone said softly. He stared the boy down until Jack turned to his mother.

"Sorry, Ma."

She nodded and tears filled her eyes, guessing he didn't mean the words. Oh, Lord, she had a feeling she had a full-fledged rebellion on her hands now. Her boys had argued with her about not wanting to leave, even if Jack was angry with Stone. The boy hadn't changed his mind about his wish to stay at the ranch.

She gave Stone a small smile. "Thanks again for all you've done."

Chris whined, "But, Mom. Stone was going to take us riding tomorrow. And he said we were going fishing, too!"

"Another time we'll go, Chris," Stone said. Stone looked at Jack. "You've got a lot of thinking to do. Do yourself a favor and stay out of trouble."

Jack shrugged Stone off and stalked toward the car.

Stone turned to Gina and took her hands in his. "Call if you need anything. Any time, day, or night, I'm here for you."

"Thanks. You've already done so much, offering us a place to stay and all."

"I meant with Jack. Believe me, Gina, I've been where he is before I learned my lesson."

"How did you learn?"

"I was arrested more than a few times in my early teen years, tossed into juvenile detention—until my uncle entered my life and gave my mom a much—needed hand, not to mention saving me from a possible life in prison."

Gina gasped at this revelation. There were a lot of hidden layers in Stone, she realized. She'd love to get to know him better, but she couldn't do it. She guessed he'd be as controlling as Charlie had been, but perhaps friendship between them was a possibility. Impossible. She knew Stone well enough to know he wouldn't be her friend because she had a strong suspicion his feelings for her were stronger than that. Unfortunately, her feelings were growing stronger for him every day.

Gina, Jack, and Chris climbed into the car and she started the engine. She put the car in reverse but kept her foot on the brake when Stone leaned into her open window.

"Thanks for the dance lessons, but I don't think I've got it all down yet. Can you come out next weekend?"

"Yes!" Chris shouted.

"You dance just fine, Stone."

"You haven't taught me how to two-step yet."

She still found it hard to believe a native Texan didn't know how to two-step. "How about next Friday, after work?"

Stone rubbed his neck. "Well, you know, Saturday would be better."

"We can accomplish what we need to after I'm through with work on Friday. Be at my office at five. I think just a few more lessons and you can start courting. Truthfully, there were little changes I could suggest for you. You're a fine man, Stone Mitchell, and you require no help in the image department, believe me," she said dryly.

Stone narrowed his eyes. "I already told you that Rachel wasn't the woman for me."

She didn't reply but backed around in the big open space then drove down the driveway. All the way home her boys remained mutinously silent.

CHAPTER ELEVEN

G ina grimaced at the turkey sandwich with lettuce and tomato slices sitting on top of the current proposal on her desk that she'd been sweating over all morning.

"You've got to eat," Ruby said, standing over her with her hands on her hips.

Gina sank against the back of her chair and glared at her secretary, also her best friend, when she reached out and tucked a paper napkin into the collar of Gina's white blouse. Gina yanked it out as soon as Ruby moved away.

Ruby sighed. "I'm disappointed that you've allowed a man to do this to you." She scowled. "If you want that man you've got to go after him, not starve yourself to death."

"You think I'm dieting because of Stone Mitchell?" Gina scoffed. "Not a chance."

Ruby gnawed on her wad of gum, then reached inside a drawer and pulled out a crumpled newspaper. "Then why in the hell do you have this paper with his picture in your drawer? Do you think I haven't seen you dig this out countless times a day for a month and look at him with big cow-eyes? Snap out of it!"

Gina sniffed. "That's his neighbor with him in that picture. I guess he decided she was the woman for him, after all."

Ruby looked closely at the photograph. "Huh. How in the heck can you tell? It looks to me like she's just giving him a trophy at a rodeo." Ruby traced the fine print with a perfect shaped red-lacquered fingernail. "It says so right here." She grinned at Gina. "Besides, there's this new guy I think would be perfect for you, and—"

Admittedly, Gina was stunned to discover the recent picture since she'd had no idea Stone had ever been involved in the rodeo circuit. "Enough!" Gina came swiftly to her feet and smacked her hands over her ears. "Just leave me alone, Ruby!"

Ruby snapped her gum furiously. "You're serious, aren't you?"

Gina immediately regretted her outburst. She crumpled into her seat, slumped over her desk, and laid her head down on her folded arms. Now, as sadness overwhelmed her, she decided she should have had her cry over the blasted man a month ago when she'd left Falcon's Ridge. Her sadness hadn't diminished but had only gotten worse. She'd given him two more dance lessons and had accepted the final payment from him. As far as she was concerned, she'd made few improvements to the man; he'd already been near-perfect.

Gina lifted her head and turned swollen red eyes on her secretary. "I never thought I'd say this, but I miss the guy."

"This is coming from the independent, liberated woman I know and love? Why don't you call him then? As a matter of fact, I've been sort of wondering why he hasn't called you."

"He has called, but with caller I.D. I've been able to dodge him, although the boys have talked to him often enough."

"I'm surprised he hasn't been more persistent."

She muttered, "So am I."

"Look, you've got to decide what you want from him. One minute you're dodging his calls, in the next you're sobbing that you miss him. Make up your mind!"

Gina sniffed. "I'll never forget him. Never."

"Gee. You talk as though the guy's dead," Ruby said, thoroughly vexed. "So, tell me this, why did you leave him if you cared about him so much?"

"At the time, I felt I was growing too dependent on him, especially where Jack was concerned."

"Being dependent isn't a crime, Gina. Call him."

Gina sniffed and raised her chin. "If he wanted to see me, he would have called."

"You said he had been calling."

"Yes, but I did answer the last few times and he asked for one of the boys, not me. And now I don't know how to break the ice between us."

"Okay, but you've got to stop carrying this infernal torch, and I know just the way to do it."

"Oh, Ruby," Gina groaned, "I'm not interested in a blind date or getting involved with another man."

"Did you hear me even mention the word 'involvement'? I'm just talking about a little date. You go out to dinner with a nice man and take in a movie. No pressure."

"A good time for a lot of men isn't my idea of fun," Gina said dryly, wiping her eyes on the sleeve of her blouse.

"The guy I'm thinking of is different. So, how about it?"

Gina raised her eyebrows. "How about what?"

"Doubling with me and my guy."

Gina saw the excitement in Ruby's eyes. "Tell me a little something about him first."

"He's fantastic and a perfect gentleman. He's just got one itsy, bitsy flaw."

"What is it?" Gina asked warily.

Ruby mumbled, "He's a cowboy with his own spread."

Gina dropped her head on her desk again and groaned, "Heaven help me." While Ruby was her employee, she was also her good friend who looked out for her.

"Well, this is Texas, after all. So you'll go out with him?" Ruby asked hopefully.

Gina raised her head and gave her secretary a baleful look. "What have I got to lose? But the first time the guy lays a hand on me so help me, Ruby, I'll brain him."

"Don't worry about that. I'll tell him you're real shy."

"Yeah, right," Gina replied, unconvinced.

The following Saturday, as Gina sat beside her date, an enormous cowboy named Bruce Frederickson, she decided she was going to tar and feather Ruby. She grimaced when he jabbed her with his elbow, apologized profusely then wound his arm tightly around her shoulders. She tried moving away but she wasn't able to budge so much as an inch. It didn't help that the Hopkins Arena seats were so close together, either.

She couldn't deny that her date was a knockout. Gina thought he could likely make a career modeling for toothpaste commercials. He was a bit shy in the intelligence department, but he had a real zest for life. He was enthusiastic and fun, and he owned a small ranch south of San Antonio that, as it turned out, was not too far from Falcon's Ridge.

After living in Texas for nine years Gina was finally seeing her first rodeo. It was great entertainment, but tense, especially after seeing a cowboy fall off an enraged bull moments ago, coming close to being gorged.

The Cattlemen's Association sponsored the rodeo and plenty of local competitors had entered. The next contestant was announced just as Gina tipped back her head to take a sip of light beer from a plastic cup. She choked when she heard Stone Mitchell's name announced. Ruby met Gina's wide-eyed look around Bruce's back and with a shrug muttered, "How in the hell was I to know?"

Gina looked into the center of the ring just as a cow raced out of the paddock. Stone followed on horseback, twirling a lasso above his head. She could see, like the other contestants, his rope was tied and coiled several times around the horn of the saddle, which allowed him to release as much rope as he needed.

Stone wasn't the oldest competitor, but close to it she decided as she focused a greedy gaze on his agile, strong body. He managed to control his horse, rope the steer, vault from his horse, and tie down the cow within seconds. Since he was the last competitor in this particular event, his time was announced, and he took second place.

Gina grinned and applauded with the other spectators when he strode out and received the second-place trophy. He returned to the stands, climbed the stairs until he reached the third row where a tall, willowy blonde stood up and threw her arms around him.

Gina got all teary-eyed when he reciprocated the embrace, literally lifting the beautiful woman off her feet and into his arms. Gina immediately recognized Stone's neighbor, Rachel Williams, from the newspaper clipping in her desk.

Bruce applauded. "That old Stoney, he's something else, isn't he?"

She tried to keep her voice casual. "You know Stone Mitchell?"

"Hell, yes! We go way back to when I worked his uncle's ranch with him on weekends. Our ranches are close together."

Gina turned and searched the stands for Stone, disappointed when she found no sign of him. The rodeo soon ended, and the crowd filed out of the arena. Bruce held Gina's hand until the press of the crowd separated them. She heard him call out, "Gina! Keep comin' straight ahead. I'll meet you at the door on the far right."

"Okay," she replied, shouting over the noise, even as unwanted thoughts entered her mind. Stone wouldn't have lost her in the crowd.

She maneuvered as best she could, unable to see much of anything due to her height disadvantage when she suddenly bumped into a wall. Raising her eyes she focused on a broad chest clothed in chambray. It wasn't a wall, but a man, and a fair-sized one at that. Her eyes moved higher, settled on a red bandanna tied around a strong neck.

Gina squeaked when the man grasped her shoulders and kept her in place as folks streamed around them. She glanced higher and gasped, stunned to see Stone intently staring down at her. Her gaze lowered to his beard, which had grown thick and bushy since his trim.

"How are you?" she asked breathlessly, placing a hand on his forearm.

"Fine…now," he murmured, slowly gathering her into his arms, giving her lots of time to stop him. When she didn't, he held her close, dark eyes boring into hers. She relaxed in his arms and wanton that she was, she tilted her chin up and offered her lips to him. Lord, she didn't know what she'd do if he turned away.

He lowered his head, gave her a tentative kiss, which grew fiercer the longer his lips stayed on hers. Both of his arms were wound tight around her waist, her breasts crushed against his stomach. His tongue darted and swirled inside her mouth. Momentarily, she was lost in the exquisite sensation of his kiss until she finally came to her senses and tore her lips away.

He scowled as he stepped back, and his gaze swept her body from head to toe. "What in the hell happened to you?"

She looked at him a moment, perplexed, until he squeezed her waist.

"You've lost weight."

Gina couldn't very well tell him she'd been pining for him, so she said the first thing to enter her mind. "I had the flu last week." This was the truth, although she hadn't lost a pound from being ill.

"A body doesn't lose that much weight from the flu." He lifted his gaze and swept the area around them before turning to stare at her again. "Are the boys with you?"

She shook her head. "I'm here with Ruby, and a few friends of hers. The boys talk about you a lot."

He leveled his dark eyes on hers. "What about you?"

"Look, Stone, you think I ran out on you, don't you?"

He scowled, nodded curtly.

"Well, I didn't."

"Could have fooled me. Every time I called your house you avoided me."

"I just didn't want you having to involve yourself in my problems with Jack. I need to handle my sons my way."

"I said it before and I'll say it again, I was only trying to help because of my own past experiences."

She arched one eyebrow. "Still, it doesn't change the fact I need to be able to live my own life the way I see fit. I need to make my own decisions and live with my mistakes."

"When can I see you?" he murmured.

Now. Forever! She eased away from him. "I don't know."

"You just said…"

"What about Rachel Williams?"

"What about her?"

Gina said dryly, "It was hard to miss her enthusiasm in the stands after you took second place. That was Rachel with you, wasn't it?"

"Yeah, but how did you know? You've never met her."

She blushed. "I saw your picture in the newspaper recently, accepting a trophy from her at another rodeo."

Stone grinned. "If I didn't know better, I'd think you were jealous."

Gina's cheeks heated and she covered them with her hands. She looked away from him, praying he hadn't seen her wearing her heart on her sleeve. She had no idea how to reply and she breathed in relief when she heard a booming voice echoing through the hallway.

"Hey, old buddy. You found my girl. How in the hell are you, Stone?"

Bruce grabbed Stone up in a big bear hug, released him and

slapped him on the back. Then he turned to Gina and pulled her close. "Isn't she something?"

"She sure is," Stone said.

Gina heard the cold tone in his voice, blushed and met the accusing look in his eyes. She bristled, thinking he had no right trying to stick her with a guilt trip. She had a right to date whom she pleased.

"This is our first date," Bruce volunteered.

Rachel suddenly appeared at Stone's side and smiled at him. "I'd lost you in the crowd."

"Sorry," Stone said, returning her smile.

Gina noticed his friendly attitude toward Rachel, but it was just that, friendly, and she relaxed.

Rachel stared at Gina and Bruce. "Friends of yours?"

Stone made short work of the introductions before grasping Rachel's elbow. He reached out and shook Bruce's hand. "Good to see you, Bruce. You take real good care of Ms. Liberatti."

Bruce grinned and twitched his eyebrows. "I plan on it."

Stone added, "Good seeing you, Gina."

"You too," she replied faintly. "I'll tell the boys I saw you."

"Do that. And drive them out to the ranch some time."

"I will," she promised.

Later, after Stone dropped Rachel off at her place, he thought about Gina and Bruce. He knew they must have met recently since it had only been four weeks since he'd last seen Gina, though it had felt longer. Just the thought of Gina out with another guy really frosted him. But he took comfort in the fact she had missed him.

From her words and actions at the rodeo, the glazed look in her eyes, the touch of her hand on him and, of course, her acceptance of his kiss told him she'd missed him. She wanted him. While he'd never been on the receiving end of genuine love from a woman, he had a strong hunch Gina was in love with him. But she was being careful— likely because she was gun shy about jumping into marriage again.

It was time he took action because he was definitely in love with Gina. One way or another she'd be walking down the aisle with him by Christmas. All he had to do was convince her.

———

The following Saturday, Stone spent the afternoon shopping, something he didn't do too often. But this shopping was important; it wasn't every day a man made a woman a marriage proposal. He wanted to have a ring in hand when he declared his intentions to Gina. He'd formulated a plan as to how to pop the question. It had to be a total surprise, and it had to be very romantic. Until he'd run into her at the rodeo and they shared that kiss, well, he was unsure of her feelings for him. That kiss proved he meant something to her.

He'd tossed and turned well into the night as he planned out his proposal, eventually managing to fall asleep. Sometime during the night the phone rang. With his face buried in his pillow, he blindly reached for it. Settling it against his ear, he grumbled, "This better be important."

"Stone? You awake?"

"I am now." He frowned. "Is that you, Jack?"

"Yeah. I need your help."

Stone's heart raced at the quiver in Jack's voice. "What's wrong? Where the hell are you?"

"I'm at one of the police stations in town."

"Which one?"

"The south station."

Stone thought, his old station, and added, "Go on." He flung his legs over the side of the bed and sat up with a frown.

"I was caught out past curfew."

"And?" Stone asked, knowing there was more.

Jack muttered, "And the police caught me drinking."

Stone narrowed his eyes on the clock radio, noting the time at two o'clock. "You got a problem, son. Where's your mom?"

"At home sleeping. She doesn't know I sneaked out of the house. They told me I could make one phone call. Can you get me out of here?"

Stone sat up. "I'm on my way."

He dressed quickly and headed out the door. As he drove, he made a guess as to what was going on in Jack's head. Likely, the same thoughts he'd had at fifteen. Then he recalled how he'd put his own mother through all sorts of sleepless nights with his rebellious behavior, but he hadn't had anyone else he could call, until he met his uncle.

Since the death of his mother five years ago, he'd regretted never once apologizing to her. He'd loved her, even if she wasn't a strong person. Gina was strong, and he knew why Jack hadn't called her. The boy expected Stone to be a buffer between him and his mother. Stone couldn't blame him since he guessed Gina would be furious.

But Jack had a rude awakening in store for him since Stone didn't take well to being called out of bed in the middle of the night. Driving at night the roads were clear and he made it to San Antonio in 1-3/4 hours, strode into the police station and found Jack sitting against one wall with Connor Wayne, who was dressed in his uniform. Breathing a relieved sigh, Stone thought Jack was lucky Connor caught him, and not one of the other cops, some of whom were tough to deal with he knew.

Jack fielded greetings from several officers he knew; the place was busy for a Saturday night, typical, he mused.

Connor rose when Stone approached, and they shook hands.

"Stone!" Jack shouted and shot to his feet.

Stone threw an arm around the boy's shoulder. "You know, Jack. If you were my son a trip to the woodshed would be on the agenda right about now."

Jack's face turned red and he muttered, "Don't you think I'm kind of old for that?"

"Hell, no," Stone retorted. "I'd say you deserve it, don't you?"

"Maybe." And then he shrugged and added, "Yeah, I guess."

"Is Jack a friend of yours?" Connor asked.

Stone looked at Jack. "Sit. I'll be back in a few minutes."

Jack flopped back down on the hard bench as Stone and Connor moved some distance away.

"Remember the woman whose house caught on fire?" Stone asked.

Connor nodded.

"Jack's her son. Have you called her?"

"Not yet. Although we told him he must since you aren't his legal guardian."

Stone nodded. "I'll call her once I finish chewing out Jack. By the way, who brought him in? Have any formal charges been made?"

Connor sighed. "I'd just finished my shift, around eleven, when I noticed an older model Dodge Caravan parked along the east county line. I pulled up behind it and found a boy and a girl in the front seat necking. Jack and another girl were in the back seat, humping away like there's no tomorrow. They'd drunk half a bottle of Jack Daniels. I also confiscated a minute bit of weed in a plastic bag."

"Damn," Stone murmured.

"They were charged with curfew violation, and underage drinking. Since the amount of marijuana was small, he wasn't charged with possession."

Stone stared at the floor a moment and then turned to Connor. "Who was the girl with Jack? Has she been released?"

"We released her to her mother about half an hour ago. The girl was your neighbor's fifteen-year-old daughter, Melissa Williams."

Stone groaned. "Any more good news and I might have to

celebrate," he said wryly. "I sure as hell don't want Rachel ticked off at me."

Connor gave Stone a curious look. "Why would she be mad at you? Jack isn't your boy."

"No, but Jack stayed at the ranch for a while. I introduced him to Melissa."

"So, can his mom handle him? How about his daddy?"

"His father died a year ago."

"Ah, that probably explains a few things. Well, go talk to him and then call his mom."

"Thanks, Connor."

All Stone could think was how he didn't look forward to calling Gina, but he had no choice.

Gina rushed into the police station half an hour later. She'd dragged Chris along since she didn't trust him enough to leave him home alone after setting the house afire. She'd told him to stay put in the car, with the doors locked.

Dressed in a snug, short jean skirt and peasant top, Stone guessed she'd tossed on the clothes. Her hair was half up and half down and windblown. To Stone's mind she looked beautiful. He smiled when he saw her bright pink flip-flops.

She found Jack slumped on the bench, and once she reached him, she cupped the back of his head, pulled him against her stomach and surrounded him with her arms. For once he didn't resist her embrace.

"What happened?" she whispered against his hair.

Jack moved back and explained the night's happenings.

Gina was stunned. "Drinking and drugs? Why in the world are you doing these things? Who were you with?"

"Melissa Williams, Sam Folly and his girl."

"I've never heard you mention a Melissa. Does she go to your school?"

"No. She goes to Wakefield High."

"Isn't that out Stone's way?"

Jack's cheeks reddened. "She's Stone's neighbor. Remember the day you crossed that rattler? That's Melissa."

She scowled and asked in a rigid tone, "Why did you do it? You sneaked out of the house after I'd gone to bed then?" When he didn't reply she snapped, "Answer me, young man."

Jack's chin jutted out and he swore, "Damn it, Mom, stop treating me like a little kid! I'm almost a man."

Gina hardly thought a fifteen-year-old a man. "You listen to me. What you did was not a sign of maturity, but foolish and irresponsible, not to mention illegal. This behavior has to stop!"

"If you'd let us stay at the ranch with Stone, I wouldn't have done any of this!" he shouted.

Gina narrowed her eyes. "Are you telling me you broke the law on purpose, thinking I'd allow you to live at Falcon's Ridge? Which holds no water since Stone caught you with marijuana at the ranch. Don't use not being able to stay at the ranch as an excuse!"

Stone ambled over and looked between the two of them. "Settle down," he murmured.

Gina eyed Stone. "How did you know about this?"

"Jack called me before he called you."

She felt utterly betrayed by the news and she turned back to Jack. "Why did you call Mister Mitchell?"

Jack shrugged and kept his eyes on his feet.

"Tell her," Stone ordered.

Jack looked at Gina with tear-filled eyes. "'Cause I was afraid to tell you. You wouldn't have understood. I've tried talking to you about stuff even before we ever met Stone, but I haven't been able to do it."

"Yet you can confide in a stranger?" Gina said, her voice trembling.

"Come on, Mom. Stone's no stranger."

Gina knew that Jack related to Stone in a way she couldn't. She also knew, in some ways, she couldn't compete with Stone with regards to her son. She shook her head and pinned Jack with a disappointed look. "What am I going to do with you?"

Jack slumped in his seat and wouldn't meet her eyes or offer a reply.

Gina met Stone's sober expression. "Thank you. I'm sorry he dragged you out of bed in the middle of the night and you had to drive all that way."

"No need to thank me. I'm glad I could help."

"What do I have to do to get him out of here and take him home?"

"I could use a cup of coffee. Come with me and we'll talk about it."

Jack started rising from the bench when Stone said, "Stay put. We'll be back in a few minutes."

The boy sighed and slouched back into his seat.

Stone guided Gina to a coffee dispenser. He fed coins into the machine and it automatically poured them each a cup. The stuff was black and sort of thick and syrupy appearing, but in the middle of the night it tasted like manna from heaven, Stone knew.

"You met Connor Wayne, remember?" At her nod he added, "He's a friend of mine who happened to find the kids and brought them in since it was after curfew. He said Jack would need to appear in court for the curfew violation. He got him off the possession charge since he found only a trace of weed. He'll also be required to go to counseling for the booze."

He took her elbow and led her to another bench. They sat down, side by side and drank their coffee in silence.

Finally, Gina said, "He's been quiet and despondent ever since we left the ranch. It's hard to believe that the short time we stayed with you made such an impression on him, but it did. I suggested he needed to see a counselor, but he wouldn't go."

"Did he ever tell you anything about what was bothering him?"

In a strangled tone, she replied, "He said he needed a dad."

Stone wasn't successful at concealing his surprised expression.

She gave him a wry look. "I know. That's been Chris's lament all along. I was every bit as surprised as you that Jack felt the same way."

"Well, now he won't have a choice about seeing a counselor," Stone said. "How have you been handling him? He hasn't gotten aggressive with you, has he?"

"He'd never lay a hand on me if that's what you're asking. I tried talking sense into him, but as you can see, words haven't worked. He started hanging with a fast crowd, too, and he refuses to bring them home for me to meet them."

"Who are these friends?"

"All I get are first names, including the two kids in the car with him this evening. Most of the kids' names aren't authentic, anyway. Many of them seem to have nicknames, and they all seem to have pagers."

"Not the new cell phones?" Stone asked.

She shook her head. "Nope, I know pagers are going out of style but many of the kids still use them. Can you believe it? Nobody gives out a home phone number anymore. It's 'call my pager and I'll call you back.' Believe me, it's hard figuring out the identities of these friends."

It was likely some of these friends were Jack's drug connections, Stone mused. "How does he react when you tell him he can't leave the house with them?"

"He stays put, although I have to wonder how many times he's sneaked out in the middle of the night. I'm confident he'll stay out of trouble from now on now that the legal system is involved."

Stone scowled. "You can't expect the police to do your job for you, Gina. You've got to enforce discipline. Cut him off from the group if you feel they're a bad influence on him."

"Easier said than done. I've tried grounding him and he just grows more distant and resentful. I've never been very firm with him, I guess, mostly because I detest confrontation and I hate being the bad guy."

"Was your husband the disciplinarian, Gina?"

She nodded. "His word meant something to Jack." She sighed. "Although mine did too while Charlie had been alive. Now that I have support, I'm hoping Jack will mend his ways. He won't have a choice."

Stone said, "I can think of a way to curtail his activities. Allow him to return to the ranch with me. I'll keep him out of trouble by working him hard, and he'll earn a wage, besides."

She came to her feet. "I appreciate your offer, but you know I can't accept."

"Sure you can," he said, rising as well. "Don't be stubborn about this. He needs help."

"I'm his mother and I'll be the one to decide what he needs," she said stiffly. "Besides, what good would it do putting him in closer proximity to Melissa?"

"I'll be able to keep an eye on him since he'd be with me every waking minute of the day. And I'm a light sleeper so I'd hear him if he tried to sneak out during the night. He did great at the ranch—Chris, too. If Jack truly likes Melissa, then I'll keep an eagle-eye on the two of them if I ever find them together."

She shook her head. "I need to handle my sons my way, Stone. Good night, and I'm sorry Jack interrupted your sleep, and I appreciate you answering his call for help."

She swept across the station to Jack's side.

Connor joined Stone. They sat down on the bench, their eyes riveted on Gina.

"So, that's the mom," Connor said. "She's—"

"Don't say it," Stone warned.

CHAPTER TWELVE

"— A real heartbreaker. How long have you known her?"

"About a month." He looked at Connor. "I know you're thinking that's not long, but I plan on asking her to marry me."

Connor laughed. "You're kidding. Right?"

Stone snapped, "I'm dead serious."

Connor held up his hands. "Hey, I didn't mean anything by that. I mean, she's a hell of a looker, but you've always been cautious in the past about women. And you hardly know this one. Why her?"

"It feels right." He tapped his chest in the approximate location of his heart. "Right here. I can't explain it. I've never fallen so hard, so fast for a woman, but I've got to be careful with her and not rush things between us. Her husband died just a year ago. I don't think she's ready to make any commitments yet." He shook his head and added, "I'd planned on asking her to marry me tomorrow, but I'll have to wait a while. She's dealing with problems with Jack so her mind's focused on him—certainly not on getting married."

"How did you say you met her?"

"She's an image consultant, owns a place called Smooth Edges here in town. I hired her to advise me on making changes in myself in order to find my future wife."

"An image consultant, huh?" Connor said. He shook his head. "What ever happened to being satisfied with who and what you are?"

Stone frowned. "You know I'm not Prince Galahad with this scar. I thought she could help make some improvements in me... without having to shave off the beard. That way, when I found a woman to court, she'd overlook my whiskers. So far, she's taught me how to dance and took me to some fancy barber for this haircut."

Connor grinned. "It looks the same as always, man."

"It's grown out now," he muttered. "Haven't had a chance to get a trim."

"She sounds like a nice woman. Have you told her about your past career as a ranger?"

Stone shook his head. "Just a little, but I'll tell her all soon."

"If she's as great as you've said, hopefully she'll see the good in you. And leaving the force was the right thing for you to do. The thing is, Stone, you can't be bullheaded with her."

"What do you mean?" Stone growled.

"You've got a tremendous stubborn streak about you and antiquated ideas with regards to women, not to mention that Heather left you two years ago because you were too protective, demanding and over-bearing."

"There's nothing wrong with having good, solid values about women, Connor. And I sure as hell can't help my protective streak, either. And you should talk! Didn't your last woman leave you because of your own demands?"

"She did, but I managed to talk her into coming back," Connor said, a smile on his face. He shrugged. "You know I hate living alone. Besides, I think Liz and I are finally on the same track. We're getting married in six months."

Stone's laughter filled the police station. When he finally settled down, he focused on his friend's ruddy complexion. "How in the hell did you manage that? You two fought like crazy when you were together."

"I was willing to make some compromises."

To Stone's mind that meant his friend had found the woman of his life because Connor never compromised. He shook his friend's hand. "Good luck. And I'd better be invited to the nuptials."

"Uh, haven't gotten as far as telling you but you're going to be my best man."

Stone slapped Connor's back and gulped down the lump in his throat. "I'd be proud to be your best man, friend. See you later."

He strode away and thought about Connor and Liz, praying he'd find the same happiness soon. He stopped outside the police station when he saw Gina and Jack at the bottom of the steps. The sky was starting to lighten so he had a good view of them.

"Think about my offer, Gina," he called out.

Gina paused on the sidewalk and looked up at Stone, opened her mouth when Jack interrupted.

"What offer?"

Stone knew he was asking for trouble from Gina when he said, "I told your mom you could stay with me at Falcon's Ridge."

"Yes!" Jack shouted before grabbing Gina up in a bear hug.

She gave Stone a wide-eyed look then reluctantly pulled out of Jack's arms. "I said no. Besides, school begins in a month."

"We've a high school nearby. Wakefield High is just thirty minutes from the ranch."

She shook her head then looked at Jack. "I'll be in the car."

Jack and Stone followed slowly behind her as she headed purposefully down the street. Jack grumbled beneath his breath, his gaze riveted on Gina's curvy ass clad in a tight skirt.

"She'll come around," Stone said. "Sooner or later. Meantime, give her a break."

Jack blushed under Stone's censorious look. "Can I come and stay with you next summer?"

Stone had every intention of having Gina with him by Christmas, never mind summer. "If your mom agrees. You may not think so, but she needs you now."

Jack sighed. "I know, but it would be a heck of a lot easier on me if she got married again. Then she'd leave me alone."

Stone chuckled. "Somehow I think she'd still keep an eye out for you. I'll call you this weekend. Maybe she'll let me come over. Before you leave, I've some advice for you."

Jack groaned and rolled his eyes.

"I don't want to hear that. Now listen to me."

"You're not going to lecture me too, are you?"

"No. But if you don't shape up things could turn real ugly for you. I've first-hand experience with rebellion, Jack." He held up a palm. "No, I'm not going to explain myself to you now, but suffice it to say I learned from my mistakes. I hope you do, too."

Stone stopped beside Gina's car, leaned down, and peered inside and Jack let himself into the front passenger seat.

Chris grinned at Stone from the back seat. "Hi ya, Stone."

"You coming out to the ranch soon, buddy?"

"You bet!" Chris shouted, then said, "Can we, Mom? Can we?"

"Soon," was all Gina said.

Stone looked at her. "Any time you want, you're welcome to visit. You don't need an invitation."

She nodded, put the car into drive and drove away.

Stone watched Gina leave, convinced more than ever that proposing marriage sooner than later would benefit all of them. He frowned then as he thought about what an independent creature Gina was, yet he couldn't envision her turning him down.

Vacations are wonderful for kids, but hell on parents Gina decided as she pulled into the Bexar County Courthouse parking lot on this last sweltering day in August. School would begin in a week, which meant Jack, thankfully, would be occupied much of the day. She'd left Chris with Kelsey Adams, a teenager down the street, even though he'd protested he was old enough to stay by himself.

She'd been called to the police station twice more in as many weeks. The last time Jack had been hauled in was for shoplifting—condoms, of all things! She finally had to face reality; her fifteen-year-old son was no longer an innocent.

Sleep had become a lost art for her, and she could have sworn she had at least two more gray hairs since she last checked. Now she worried what the courts would do with Jack, knowing there was the possibility he could be placed in a juvenile detention facility.

Stone offered to pick up Jack at home and drive him to the court hearing since she had a client appointment. Arriving at the courthouse, she emptied her purse of her cell phone and car keys and passed them to the court attendant, then slipped inside the hearing room. She found Jack flanked by Stone on one side, and on the other sat his court-appointed attorney, Jerome Mavison.

Suspicion entered her mind as she wondered why they'd allowed Stone into the hearing room since he wasn't Jack's parent. She had a hunch she'd find out shortly. Of course, his having been in law enforcement might have something to do with it. He had connections. She took the chair next to Stone.

"Now, don't worry about a thing." Stone took her hand in his, squeezed and released it.

She gave him a bittersweet smile. "Tough thing to ask me to do."

Connor Wayne sank into a seat in the row behind them. He leaned forward and whispered in Stone's ear. Gina strained to hear their conversation but only caught an occasional word or two, and then they laughed companionably. There was something wrong about the lack of tension in either man although her own apprehension was so tangible even a stranger would have noticed it. Stone was up to something.

Wayne left as soon as the judge entered and everyone in the hearing room rose. Judge Madeline Olufson was a tall, blonde woman of Swedish descent, and a decidedly commanding figure as she stood behind the heavy mahogany desk. She stared sternly at Jack from behind a pair of wire-rimmed glasses.

Gina had to give the judge credit for not mincing words as she rapidly ticked off her son's offenses. Jack wisely pled guilty on all counts. Once all the formalities were taken care of, Judge Olufson said, "Jack, your mom has tried hard to keep you leashed, but you've proven recalcitrant time and time again. And, from what I gather, you haven't been repentant. I'll tell you now, young man, you're running with the wrong crowd, and from now on your freedom will be curtailed."

Gina waited with bated breath for Jack's sentence and was stunned when she heard the judgment.

"You've one hundred hours of community service hours to perform, some of it manual labor to work off over the next several months. The only way that I can see you completing the hours, in a timely fashion, is to place you within a facility where you'll live, attend school, and work the hours off after school. This will also afford you the opportunity to re-evaluate your friendships while you're away from them."

"We've a number of institutions in this county where we could place you, for a substantial charge to your mother. Unfortunately, at this time, there are no openings in any of them."

Gina gulped down the lump in her throat. They couldn't lock him up—he had to come home with her!

The judge continued, "You're a very fortunate young man, Jack, because we've found a place for you, free of charge."

Gina's eyes filled with tears when she glimpsed the shocked look on her son's face. She hurt for him, but perhaps he'd finally learn his lesson.

"Bexar County has determined that you'll work off your community service hours at Falcon's Ridge Ranch, under Mister Mitchell's supervision."

Jack jabbed the air with one fist. "Yes!"

Gina felt as though someone had punched her.

"Quiet," the judge ordered. "You'll be supervised by Mister Mitchell, who's offered to accommodate you under the circumstances. Do you understand your sentence, Jack?"

Jack nodded eagerly, his lips forming all sorts of interesting and rather comical shapes as he tried concealing his jubilation. He met Stone's warning look, then sobered and straightened in his chair.

"The court stenographer cannot see you nodding your head, young man."

"Yes!" Jack replied.

Gina raised her hand. "Your Honor?"

"Yes, Ms. Liberatti." The judge turned to the stenographer. "Off the record, Miss Johnson."

"How is Mister Mitchell qualified to care for my son? He's not a parent, he's not a probation officer nor is he married and the distance from our home to the ranch will make it nearly impossible for me to visit during the week days that I work."

"Your son is in a very vulnerable position at the moment and needs close supervision. Do you work week-ends, Ms. Liberatti?"

"Not usually," Gina said softly.

"You may visit your son then. As to Mister Mitchell's qualifications as a probation officer, you'll be comforted to know that law enforcement had been his line of work for a number of years. He's also a certified foster parent in the county."

Jack's eyes widened on Stone. "You were a cop?"

"I'm not finished, young man," Judge Olufson said sternly, "but I'll answer your question. Mister Mitchell used to be one of the state's finest Texas Rangers until he retired five years ago." She smiled. "You'll be in safe hands."

"Anything else we need to clear up?" she asked, staring around the hearing room. When no one replied she turned back to Jack. "This coming weekend, you will pack your bags and move to Falcon's Ridge." She looked at Gina and added, "You will need to go down to the high school in Crescent City, the high school closest to the ranch and register him for school." Her gaze returned to Jack. "On a weekly basis, Mister Mitchell will sign off the hours you've completed of your sentence. You have until March 1st to complete your hours. Is that clear?"

"Yes, ma'am."

"Good. Once the hours are completed, you'll return home, on probation of course, until the next hearing which you'll be receiving notice of shortly but won't occur until after you've completed probation. You are also required to attend school faithfully during this time, maintain at minimum, average grades and stay law-abiding. That's it folks. Good luck, Jack. Follow the rules and you'll have no more problems."

Everyone stood up as Judge Olufson left the room. Stone and Jack turned to Mavison and thanked him. Once Mavison left Jack turned to his mother.

"Thanks, Mom."

"For what?" she snapped as she came to her feet. Jack's complexion reddened and she added, "I've the distinct impression you've engineered this entire string of bad behavior for the outcome you were awarded, and don't play dumb with me. You know precisely what I'm talking about."

When Jack didn't reply but hung his head, Gina turned a teary-eyed look on Stone. "As for you, I have no words to describe what I feel toward you at the moment." She swung around to Jack again. "You'll do all your own packing since I have no idea what all you want to take with you to the ranch."

Jack's eyes widened. "Aren't you coming too, Mom? And what about Chris?"

"I don't think my presence would benefit your rehabilitation.

Chris and I will visit on weekends, as the judge suggested. Thank Stone for stepping in and helping you. I'll meet you at the car."

She left and Stone and Jack followed slowly behind. Stone draped an arm around Jack's shoulders. "She's got every right to be angry with you, and I've got to admit her words make a hell of a lot of sense. Did you break the law on purpose, thinking I'd take you in?"

CHAPTER THIRTEEN

J ack shook his head but wouldn't meet Stone's eyes.

"Look at me."

Jack raised his eyes and tightened his lips.

"Did you do it on purpose?"

"No—well, a few things, maybe," he amended. "I wanted to be close to Melissa."

"So why did you break the law by stealing?"

"Because mom only gives me ten dollars allowance a week. And I couldn't afford the movies, flowers and con—" He blushed and didn't finish his sentence.

Stone finished it for him. "Why do you need protection?"

"I'm still seeing Melissa."

Stone swore vividly. "Obviously, you two are doing more than seeing each other. How do you manage to see her when she lives way the hell out by me, anyway?"

"I sneak over to her place at night after mom's gone to bed."

"How? You don't have a car."

That gave him pause, especially when he saw the guilty look on Jack's face. "You've been sneaking your mom's car out at night, haven't you?"

Jack stared at his feet.

Stone sighed. "So didn't your mom notice the gas gauge being low after you used the car?"

"Melissa gave me money to pay for gas so mom never noticed."

"Have you had driver training yet?"

"No."

"Why haven't you taken the class?"

"Mom said she couldn't afford to pay the extra car insurance. She said when I get a job to pay for it myself, she'll let me take the training."

"Sounds like a sensible plan."

"But I've no way of getting to work until I learn to drive, and then I'll need a car," he protested. "Ten dollars a week is nothing when a guy's taking out a girl."

Stone couldn't agree more.

"Right now I could get a job at one of the fast-food restaurants since they hire at fifteen. But the restaurants are over three miles away from our house."

"Do you have a bike?"

"Yeah, but the chain's broke."

"So fix it," Stone insisted.

"Don't know how." He looked at Stone hopefully. "Maybe you could show me."

"We'll bring it along to the ranch and work on it. Now, you know you won't be getting paid while working off your community service hours, don't you?"

"I sort of figured that," Jack grumbled

"There's a McDonald's about six miles from Falcon's Ridge. I know for a fact they hire at fifteen. When you're through working for me you could work a few hours a day there, like during the supper hour. And once we fix up your bike, you'll have transportation."

Jack couldn't contain his excitement. "Okay!"

"I'll speak with your mom about driver's education. I'm willing to help pay for your insurance, with the understanding that you pay part of it once you start working. Agreed?"

"For sure!" Jack said with a grin. Then frowned. "But I won't have enough money to buy a car."

"I've got a junker in the garage that needs some work. I'll work with you to get it up and running. It'll be perfect for you."

Stone noticed Gina across the street in her car, waiting. He turned to Jack. "I'm setting down ground rules right now before you park your butt on the ranch. Number one, and this goes without saying, no more shop-lifting or drugs or cigarettes."

"Yes, sir."

"I'm not kidding about this, Jack. If you don't follow the rules, I'll march you out to the barn and blister your butt. Understand?"

Jack flushed but nodded.

"And no more playing around with Melissa."

"You've no say in that," Jack said belligerently. "I love her. Besides, she wouldn't understand if we stopped…"

He reddened under Stone's appraising eyes. "You don't really want to have sex with her, do you?" Stone asked softly.

"Sure I do, but not if she keeps wanting other stuff—stuff I don't want."

Stone frowned. "What stuff is that?"

"Marriage and being committed."

Stone raised his brows. "Did she say she wanted to get married?"

Jack nodded, flushed. "I told her we're too young. Melissa is great, though. You know?"

"Melissa and Mrs. Williams are my neighbors. Melissa's mom wouldn't take kindly to you taking up with her daughter again. You two have been caught twice already."

"I know," Jack said and groaned. "When Mrs. Williams picked up Melissa at the station, she stopped and talked to me."

"And what did she say?"

"Told me to stay clear of her daughter."

"Which you haven't."

"I've seen her just a few times since we met." He sighed. "I like her a lot, but I've tried breaking up with her cause I'm not ready for everything she wants, but it's hard."

"I thought you said you love her."

"I do—no, maybe not." Jack raised his woeful gaze to Stone. "I'm confused."

Stone knew it took a lot from Jack to make that kind of confession. He was a young boy on the brink of manhood and was going through hell fighting his hormones.

A horn blared and they turned to find Gina scowling at them. Stone grinned and waved, then turned to Jack. "Do you mind if I had a little talk with Mrs. Williams? Between us maybe we can settle things down a bit between you and Melissa—like establishing a good friendship instead of a 'love-ship'. What do you say?"

Jack threw himself against Stone. Stone stumbled back and grasped the boy against him. "Whoa, there!"

"You're the best, Stone," Jack muttered against Stone's shirt.

Stone grinned then rubbed his knuckles against the top of Jack's skull. Jack laughed and pulled out of Stone's arms.

"Just so you know, it won't be easy going backwards with Melissa."

Jack shrugged his shoulders and murmured, "I know."

"See you tomorrow," Stone said. "Now get going before your mom really gets mad at us."

He watched Jack cross the street and jump into the car. Then he strode to his own vehicle. As he put the car into gear and merged into traffic, he thought over his plan for wooing Gina. He grinned, knowing she wouldn't be able to resist him. His smile slipped then when he thought about how he'd have to tell her about his past career, and more details about his battle wounds which weren't a pretty sight. One thing at a time...

After work Friday, Gina drove out to Falcon's Ridge with Chris and Jack and Jack's clothing and other items—lots of other items.

While he dragged his clothing and lots of other stuff to the room assigned to him, Gina waited at the back door for him to return, to say goodbye.

"Gina, stay for supper," Marguerite said.

Gina shook her head. "I have to get back home with Chris but thank you."

Marguerite gave her a worried look. "Just supper. You have to eat."

She opened her mouth to decline once more when she heard Stone's steps from behind her. Gina moved to the side to let him pass into the house. He stopped beside her.

"Hi," he said. "Staying for supper, aren't you?"

"Thank you, but not this time."

"Aw, come on, Mom," Chris whined. "Marguerite has her tacos and you know how much I like them."

"I already thawed out chicken for supper."

"I'm sick of chicken. I want tacos," Chris whined.

"Come here," she said, a warning tone in her voice.

He stumbled over to her, reluctantly, when Stone spoke.

"It's just tacos, Gina."

She bit her lip a moment, her gaze flitting between Stone and Marguerite. "Okay, thank you," she said softly.

Chris whooped and took his place at the table.

"Wash up first, Chris," Stone directed.

Gina wasn't surprised when Chris launched out of his seat and took his place at the sink as she thought about how he'd argue with her when she'd ask him to do the same thing. And usually she would ask and even include a please and got arguments, while all Stone had to do was tell the boys to do something and they did it.

Gina watched him wash his hands, kicking herself for noticing how taut his butt was clad in those well-worn jeans he favored. His legs were strong and long, his shoulders wide—wide enough to take on the world she guessed, then sighed.

What was it with this guy? Or was it men in general? Why did her sons argue with her and not with Stone? Was it because he was a novelty to them? She knew they loved the ranch but still…was it because Stone was a guy—and heavens she knew how much they missed their dad.

Soon they sat down at the kitchen table to eat. She listened to conversation between her sons, Stone and Marguerite, but kept silent.

Truth be told, she was jealous of Jack's adoration of Stone. She couldn't recall when her son had looked at her the same way—with absolute adoration. Well, perhaps when he was three, but not in recent years. She turned a jaundiced eye on Stone, wondering how many other secrets he'd kept from her; for instance, the fact he was a certified foster parent in Bexar County. And a former Texas Ranger?

After consuming half a taco, she set it down. She simply had no appetite.

"Eat up, Gina," Marguerite scolded. "A good wind could pick you up and carry you away. You've lost weight since you left the ranch."

"I'm not all that hungry."

When she saw Chris finish his taco, she rose from the table and flicked her eyes over the foursome.

"If you'll excuse me, it's time for us to go home. And thanks for dinner, Marguerite."

She turned away but stopped at Stone's soft statement.

"Gina? Can I have a word with you?"

Never had she met a man who liked to talk as much as Stone. She narrowed her eyes on him, noting the determined look in his eye.

"About what?"

"I've something very important to tell you, and it can't wait any longer. I should have told you sooner."

Biting her lip, she decided that while she wanted to hear about his past—his life—she was simply not up for it tonight.

"I'm tired," she said wearily, "but you're right. We should talk. But not tonight."

She saw Stone's smile slip and he scowled at her as he came around the table toward her.

"You know, Miz Liberatti, you can't always have things your way. I'd really like to talk now. It won't take long."

Gina tilted her chin up and said coolly, "You're asking me to compromise with you, is that it?" At his curt nod she added, "Don't you dare talk to me about compromising. During my marriage, I wrote the book on it!" She looked at her youngest. "Let's go, Chris. Jack, we'll see you next weekend."

She snatched up her plate, glass and utensils and carried them to the sink, aware of the uncomfortable silence. Marguerite had run a full sink of steamy water to rinse the dishes before loading them into the dishwasher. Gina scraped the remains of her dinner into the garbage disposal then slid the dishes and utensils into the sink. Then she headed for the door.

"Thank you, Marguerite. Stone. Come on, Chris."

At her car she reached out to open the door when a large hand covered her own. Gina glanced up and found Stone's imposing body beside her.

"Is this the way it's going to be between us?" he growled.

"What are you talking about? There is no *us.*" She was stunned by his anger, for in all the weeks she'd known him she'd never seen him this way.

He took her shoulders. "You mind telling me why you're so angry with me."

She looked at him, surprised. "What?"

"Ever since Jack called me the first time from the police station you've been ticked at me. Why?"

She scoffed, "You're imagining things. Why would a thing like that bother me?"

"That's what I'm wondering."

"I was grateful that you went to the station for him. It was wonderful and kind and…I wasn't just ticked off. I was royally ticked off! He should have called me first," she exploded.

"That's what I figured this was about. But you really shouldn't take it personally. Teenaged boys usually respond better to male authority."

Gina gave an impotent shriek and stomped her foot. "I think we've both said enough."

"You're sorta cute when you're mad." Stone grinned and tapped her nose

She gasped as he turned and made his way to the door, saying, "Whenever you're ready to talk more, I'll be in the family room. Or, you could call me when you arrive home, though I think we'd get more settled if you stayed put."

She fumed inside as she watched him cockily walk toward the house. He was way too smug for his own good and she stormed after him all the while aware she wasn't certain what she'd say or do.

"Mom!" Chris ran behind her. "We staying?"

"Just a few minutes longer. Go find Jack and tell him goodbye again and wait with him until I come and get you," she instructed.

"Yes!" he shouted, running past her and inside the house, ducking around Stone who held the door open.

Gina stomped toward him. As he waited for her, she could see he was trying to conceal his grin.

She stopped right next to him with a glare, her hands on her hips. "Did you call me cute?"

"Yep, sure did, darlin'."

"I'm not cute. I'm mad."

"I know."

"And I'm frustrated."

"You sure are. I can fix that."

Gina gasped then when he gathered her in his arms and lowered his head. His lips swooped down and covered her mouth as he closed the door.

There on the back stoop, he kissed her gently and Gina went limp against him. With an arm around her waist he lifted her, turned, and pressed her back against the door. Then she was lost, forgetting why she had been angry as he trailed hot kisses from her lips and down one side of her face and neck, his beard soft and ticklish. Then he bent his knees and his lips formed over one nipple, searing her skin through her white t-shirt and bra.

She was disappointed when he straightened and backed up a few steps, pulling her with him. Then he took her by surprise when he shoved one shoulder into her mid-section and hauled her over his broad shoulder.

"Stone! What do you think you're doing?" she gasped, struggling against his hold. "Put me down!"

"Not a chance," he said, patting her butt. He opened the door and shouted, "Hey, Marguerite, keep an eye on the boys for a bit while Gina and I talk, will you?"

"Sure thing, Stoney!" Marguerite called back.

Gina felt like screaming bloody murder but had no desire to make a fuss in front of her children when Jack suddenly poked his head out the back door of the house. "Stone? You're not going to—"

Gina braced her hands against Stone's broad shoulder, lifting herself to eye her son, wondering what he meant to say, noting the apprehensive expression in his eyes. Then she stilled at Stone's amazing words.

"No, I'm not going to beat her butt like I threatened to do to you if you got out of line."

"Okay," he said agreeably, and Jack grinned as he watched Stone carry her away.

That did it.

Gina shrieked and managed to knee Stone in the stomach —hard.

CHAPTER FOURTEEN

S tone ignored the knee jab and kept walking toward the barn. Gina shrieked again when he had the audacity to reach up and pat her butt again. "It may not be such a bad idea," he grumbled.

Her knee jabbed him again, harder this time.

"You want to fight, lady?" Stone asked. "We'll fight. But not where everyone can hear and see us. And then, when you've got it all out of your system and you see things my way, we'll make up. That's the best part of a relationship," he said conversationally. "Making up."

What relationship? "Damn you! Stop!"

"Don't worry, Mom," Jack called out. "Stone's real good at talking sense into folks."

"Get in the house, Jack!" Stone called out.

"Jack, no, come—" She heard the door slam shut and groaned, even as she pummeled Stone's back as he drew nearer to the barn. He yanked open one of the double doors, set her down inside, then closed and bolted the door shut. Gina wasn't a coward she told herself, still she moved further into the dark recesses, waiting for him to make the next move. Through the dimness in the tall cavernous place, she saw his eyes glimmering with impatience.

He growled, "Start hollering. Don't clam up on me now. You've been simmering inside for days now. Spit it out."

"Why would I do that?" she asked with as much dignity as she could muster as she backed slowly away from him.

"Why? It's what you've been wanting to do, isn't it?"

Gina's lower lip trembled, and tears welled in her eyes. When they started spilling down her cheeks, she heard Stone groan.

"Damn it! Don't you start bawling now," he warned.

She sobbed harder.

He headed her way and she stumbled back, turning her back on him and swiping at her cheeks.

"If I feel like crying, I will," she retorted.

He laid his hands on her shoulders and turned her around to face him. "Go ahead then," he said gently, "Cry. I guess you've the right."

Gina whirled to face him, tucked her cheek against his broad chest and gave in to the sadness that had been building up inside her over time; her futile attempts to control her rebellious son, her sadness at leaving Stone and the ranch when her boys had been so happy there, all because she was confused about her feelings for Stone.

She had a hunch he'd be popping the big question to her soon. She just didn't know how she'd reply. For the first time in her life she was accountable to only herself and her kids. No domineering fathers or husbands around to make demands of her and, in general, make her life miserable, and she enjoyed her freedom. Yet she knew it would only be a matter of time and she'd be with Stone. It was inevitable because she knew he cared for her and her boys, and she decided she cared enough about him. Maybe freedom was overrated...

After sobbing a river of tears she rubbed the top of her head against his chest. He kept his hands on her shoulders, massaged them. She sighed blissfully at their strength and warmth.

"You know what?" he asked after a while as he wound his arms around her waist.

Gina tilted her head back and stared into his eyes. "What?"

"I was pretty ticked off when you left me, and you wouldn't talk to me when I called," Stone said.

"All you had to say was I need to talk to you. Instead, you always asked for one of the boys."

He gawked at her. "I tried but you kept hanging up on me."

"That was at first. Why didn't you persist? I would have spoken to you eventually."

"Do you know what it's like always being turned down, turned away? I didn't dare approach you again. But why did you leave the ranch? Your house wasn't ready yet. You could have stayed."

"We'd been enough trouble to you." She sighed. "And I wasn't too crazy about another man trying to make the calls in mine and my sons' lives again."

"No kidding. I got the message, loud and clear. Did I ever tell you about my mother?" Stone asked.

Gina shook her head, her eyes wide, marveling at how he'd changed the subject.

"She was sick most of her life with one illness or another. I never knew my father. My childhood and adolescence weren't the best years. Mom tried hard but she was lonely and sick most of the time. And I didn't give her much leeway, especially during my early teenaged years. But later, when she got sick, I took care of her the best I could."

Gina smiled through her tears. "It comes naturally to you, doesn't it? This role of caretaker?"

He shrugged. "I guess. Maybe I've been overprotective with you, but I certainly have no intentions of cramping your style, taking your boys away or running your life."

"You could have fooled me," she said dryly. "You must try very hard from now on and not interfere. This is my life, my decisions to make, especially where Jack is concerned. I just don't want him getting his hopes up for something permanent between us."

"Why not something permanent?"

"Because it's not a good time for us to be together. Frankly, I'm not sure how I feel about you, Stone." *Liar!*

He hauled her into his arms. "Sure it's the right time. And I think you like me well enough," he said arrogantly.

She squirmed. "Didn't we just talk about no pressure?"

When he nudged her jeans-clad legs apart and settled one thigh between hers she stiffened. Then he gently shoved her against the barn's ragged wall and kissed her until she wound her arms around his neck and kissed him back. Soon they were rubbing against each other. Stone had to bend his knees in order to maintain contact with her most intimate parts. Gina went up onto her toes and then slowly lowered to her feet, time and time again, brushing against his big, hard body.

Lord, she couldn't recall ever being so close to having an orgasm while still wearing clothes. Then Stone shoved his pelvis hard against hers, pressing her into the barn wall. She groaned in pleasure and pushed back. It wasn't enough and she longed to remove all of their clothing.

"Mom? Stone? You in here?"

They parted immediately at the sound of Chris calling them. While Gina straightened her clothes, Stone headed toward the barn door. He stopped in front of Chris.

"Your mom's fine. Were you worried about her?"

Chris blushed, started shaking his head and then nodded.

Stone laughed and tousled his hair. "We've just been talking things over."

"Talkin's good," Chris stated.

Stone looked over his shoulder as Gina came up beside him. He swung an arm around her waist and pulled her against him. "Let's go inside."

Chris sped away and Gina and Stone followed. Stone squeezed

Gina's waist as they ambled across the yard. "You're not leaving yet, Gina."

She arched her brows. "Orders, again?"

"Hell, yes. And maybe one of these times you'll follow them. Now I know where Jack got that stubborn streak of his." He stopped and pulled her against him before they reached the house. He kissed her neck.

She laughed and arched away from him. "Darn it, Stone. Your whiskers tickle! Would you ever shave it off for me?"

"Never," he muttered. "As for giving orders I've learned you'll likely do the complete opposite of whatever I say, anyway. You need a lickin', lady. You know that?"

She just smiled.

He snorted. "Why must you be so contrary and independent?"

"And why must you be so controlling and over-protective?"

"Just my nature, I'm afraid. I already explained that to you."

"A lickin', huh?" she asked.

"Damned right."

She grinned. "Hmm, I've never been into all that kinky stuff, but who knows? Maybe I'm missing out on something."

His nostrils flared and he narrowed his eyes. "Don't tempt me, woman. We still have a lot more talking to do."

"You're right, like why you are no longer in law enforcement for one. But I'm too tired tonight."

"You and Chris are welcome to stay the night, you know. Any time."

"I may take you up on that."

"Ah, music to my ears."

"You are a big cliché, you know that?"

He just grinned down at her.

Gina laughed, tucked her arm through his and they walked side by side into the house. When they entered the kitchen, they passed Marguerite, who sent Gina a knowing grin. Gina settled down on the sofa in the family room, her boys sprawled on the floor at her feet.

She'd deal with Stone, one day at a time. Perhaps he'd learned that she truly meant to keep her independence, and that he'd be the one who would need to change—if he expected her to have anything to do with him. She started thinking about what he'd need to change to satisfy her and she couldn't think of one thing at the moment.

———

Gina woke the following morning to brilliant sunlight peeking between the slats of the narrow blinds, which she'd forgotten to close last night. She rolled over and squinted at the clock, stunned to see it was noon. My God! She couldn't remember when she'd slept in this late.

She sat up quickly ready to check her planner for appointments when she remembered it was Saturday. She sank back on the bed and closed her eyes. Smiling, she remembered being exhausted last night, falling asleep during a second movie they had watched, and Stone carrying her into the guestroom she'd used the first time she'd stayed at Falcon's Ridge.

Her eyes shot open again when a knock sounded on the door.

Holding the sheet to her chest she sat up halfway, balancing on one elbow as the door slowly opened. Stone stood there with a tray in his hands.

"Morning, darlin'."

"Good morning," Gina said, returning his smile, her eyes focused on the tray. "You should have woke me earlier."

"Figured you needed the sleep." Stone settled the tray on the bed across her lap, then sat down beside her.

Swiping her hair back from her forehead she said, "I was really tired, I guess. Not sleeping well lately."

They reached for the tray at the same time when it started to topple, and their hands brushed against each other. She held on while he pulled his hands away.

"I don't believe I've ever had breakfast served to me in bed. Thank you." She looked down at the tray, a frown on her brow and he laughed.

"You're welcome. As you can see, lunch, not breakfast."

Thoughts of how he'd confronted her in the barn last evening filled her mind as she picked up a spoon and took a tentative sip of what she discovered was minestrone soup. "This is wonderful."

"It's just from a can."

She met his eyes. "Stone, I…"

"Gina," he said at the same time. He inclined his head. "Ladies first."

"I'm not sure where to begin." She met his eyes and her cheeks heated under the intent look in his eyes. "Maybe a good place would be to thank you for being there for Jack. I know I wasn't very appreciative at the courthouse, and I apologize for that. I guess I suspected you engineered the courts into allowing Jack to move in with you. This made me believe you had an ulterior motive for doing so."

"That's why we need to have an honest talk. And I didn't engineer the situation."

She frowned. "I see."

He shook his head. "No, I don't think you have a clue." His eyes searched hers as he took her hands. "I care for you, Gina, you already know that."

She nodded as heat seeped into her cheeks. "The feeling is mutual. But it doesn't give you the right to interfere in my life. Although I must admit you've more tact and finesse than my father or Charlie ever possessed. They made all my decisions for me and I was helpless to stop them. I hated it and hated them for doing it. But you—you are so *nice* in your efforts to control my life. Your approach is more creative, I guess you could say, but the end result is the same. I won't allow it."

"Well, that's something in my favor, isn't it?" He gave her a devilish grin. "That I *nicely* interfere."

She scowled at him. "Actually, I believe your approach is much more dangerous to my well-being then if you were blatant about it."

"I've said this before...I'll try not to interfere." He stared at her, his eyes coursing her body before returning to her eyes. "I want you to stay here at Falcon's Ridge, you and Chris, of course. I truly am a foster parent and take kids—mostly teenaged boys here during these types of crisis. I didn't happen to have anyone with me currently so Connor Wayne recommended me to the judge. He spoke to me first about it and I agreed."

Gina's heart pranced happily and then doubts started filtering through her. She had no desire to lose her heart and soul to a man again, but she was. She continued eating, without giving him a reply—uncertain how to.

He leaned forward. "Did you hear what I said?"

She met his eyes. "I heard you, but I'd like a bit more clarification as to your intentions."

Stone stood up and paced the floor, then stopped and jammed his hands on his hips. "What I want is for you, Jack and Chris to live here...permanently."

"Now why would I want to do that when I have a house of my own?" she asked mildly. *He couldn't possibly be proposing marriage? Could he?*

"Hell, Gina. We're good together, that's why." He shoved his hair off his forehead, then stroked his beard as he paced the floor some more. "I want you to marry me."

"Marry you?" Her heart soared at his words, but then doubts entered her mind. "You're saying this because I'm the only available woman in your life, and because you'd like to marry by Christmas."

"All right, I'll admit my idea was ridiculous, but I meant what I said at the time. I'm tired of living alone. Tired of feeling lonely."

"And what about love?"

He scowled. "I hate the way folks—women in particular, toss that word around." He turned the tables on her then. "Okay." He raked his hair back. "I love you, damn it. There. I've said it, and I mean it. How about you?"

CHAPTER FIFTEEN

S he nearly screamed, *yes,* but stopped herself in time. She was attracted to him, in a primal way, but she wasn't certain she loved him. And if with time she did, could she be bound to another dominating man—one who'd try and make the hard decisions for her—one who'd run her life—even if he managed to do it in a nice way?

"You're just saying that because you've been lonely. Frankly, Stone, I'm not ready to marry again. I'm not ready to make that kind of commitment. I care for you and I enjoy our time together, when we aren't arguing, but I also enjoy my freedom."

"And I'd do nothing to infringe on your freedom, darlin'," he said. "Once I met you, I wasn't interested in Rachel, or anyone else. I want to make love to you. The whole night long, every night, for the rest of our lives."

Her eyes nearly popped out. She stifled the words running through her head; *yes, yes, yes, no!*

"I could convince you."

Gina hated his confident tone but recognized the truth of it. Her voice shook when she replied, "I know, but you won't because I don't want you to."

"I didn't want to tell you this, but Jack already knows about us. He saw us together."

Gina's face paled. "When? How?"

Stone sighed. "Remember when you stayed here after the fire? It was during one of our dance lessons in the library. Remember when I started seducing you on my desk?"

She met his eyes and her face heated up. "Oh, God." How could she forget?

"That's why I stopped us from going further. Jack saw us. I'd left the library door open. I happened to look up into the mirror hanging on the wall behind you and saw Jack's reflection."

Gina shook her head. "He couldn't have seen much since we were both still dressed."

"You're right. It was a good thing because he was angry enough at just our kissing. That kid of yours throws a mean punch."

"He hit you?" she asked, clearly shocked. "When?"

Stone grinned. "Sure did. After you went to bed I went into his room and talked with him. I would have done the same thing if I'd been in his position. The boys expect us to marry. I've heard them say so."

"It doesn't matter because I'm not ready."

"There's no such thing as the right or wrong time. That's your head talking, trying to make sense of all of this. Just follow your heart."

Softly, she asked, "And what is your heart saying?"

"It's telling me to marry you, white wedding dress, flowers, cake, preacher, the whole shebang."

He slid his hand inside the bodice opening of her nightgown and cupped her breast. Then he slid both hands down her body and grasped her hips. He pulled her down so she lay flat on the bed as he nuzzled his lips between the button-placket opening of her gown. His lips formed around one nipple and he suckled it gently.

Gina gasped and widened her eyes as he slowly eased her gown up and over her hips. She saw the blazing look of desire in his eyes then followed his hand's movement as he pulled down the zipper on his jeans.

The sound of footsteps in the hallway made them both still. A knock sounded on the door and she looked around Stone and saw the doorknob turning. She shoved against his shoulders and whispered, "Stone, stop!"

He slipped a finger to his lips. "It's all right. I locked the door. Be quiet and they'll think you're still asleep."

Gina heard footsteps fade away in the distance and she frowned. "You planned this from the moment you slipped in here with lunch, didn't you?"

"I was being cautious."

She scrambled from the bed and jammed her hands on her hips. "You were fairly confident I'd swoon into your arms, weren't you?"

"Who are you kidding, Gina?" He rose, nearly meeting her nose to nose. "You want this as much as I do. We want each other so be honest about it."

"That may be true, but I'm not ready for marriage."

"Would you settle for an exclusive relationship?"

She shook her head and slammed her eyes shut against the temptation. She scoffed, "It's easy for you to make me want you. What red-blooded woman wouldn't want a handsome man like you?"

He gawked at her a moment, then grinned. "You think I'm handsome." He took a step.

"Don't come any closer," she warned.

"Stop me," he drawled, his eyes sweeping down her body as he ambled toward her.

Before Gina could even think about moving away, he made short work of hauling her down to the bed.

Gina propped herself up on her elbows and gasped at the look on his face, blushing at his sexy, determined expression. She shivered and her eyes widened when he pulled the hem of her gown up and, ducking his head he closed in on her. She shoved a hand against the top of his head but couldn't budge him. Then she yelped, startled when his tongue unerringly found her. Soon incoherent words spewed from her mouth, her entire being focused on the most fantastic, erotic sensations she'd ever felt in her life. Her hands delved into his thick hair at the same moment her climax shook her.

Reality sank in as she came down off her high. Her eyes shot open when he settled his naked body over hers as she wondered how in the world he'd undressed so quickly.

"I feel as though I've been waiting a lifetime for you," he said, nuzzling her neck.

She gulped and wondered what in the world she was doing. What was wrong with her? Lord, hadn't she just told him she wasn't ready for an intimate relationship? But she was helpless to stop him—didn't want to. She felt him move off her and she opened her eyes. He'd moved to the other side of the bed and was rummaging inside the bedside table. He pulled open a silver packet and she blushed when he turned toward her and sheathed himself. How had she forgotten something so important? Then she asked herself how sure of her he must have been to be prepared.

Her eyes drifted from the smoldering look in his eyes to his incredibly wide chest covered with a thick mat of soft black hair. He was the most thoroughly masculine man she'd ever slept with. *Hell, he was only the second man.* She smiled in chagrin. Now he had her swearing, mentally!

She frowned as he settled himself over her. She held him off, her arms straight, her hands pressed against his chest as she said, "You're prepared."

"Now don't go thinking too much into this," he said with a gentle smile. "I'd rather not be using a goddamned thing."

Her lips trembled as she wound her arms around his neck and pulled him close, relieved by his words. "Thank you for that." Then he entered her, hard as steel and hot—oh, so very hot inside her. It was bliss; it was heavenly. She wound her legs around his waist and when he thrust inside her, her eyes filled with tears at the wonder of their beautiful mating. Then he reached down between their bodies, his eyes growing darker as he found and stroked her to the most fierce, arousing state she'd ever known. It didn't take long for her to topple into sweet oblivion again, followed by his climax.

They were drenched and panting in each other's arms, the sweaty aftermath of sex prompting Gina to think that their loving was a wonderful thing.

Charlie had been a pretty conventional guy about most things in life, including sex. Stone's technique was unique and exciting. Warmth, peace, and happiness spread through her body. She sighed as she recognized the truth; she was very much in love and she could deny it 'til snow fell in Africa, but it wouldn't change her feelings.

———

The first cloud on Gina's clear horizon appeared two days later. It was Monday morning and Stone was out and about with Jack and Chris while she enjoyed the blissful quiet, getting ready for work. She really should have gone home last night, but Stone had convinced her to stay a second night. She'd drawn the line at sharing his bed, though, which he couldn't understand at all after what they'd done in her room earlier in the day. But he understood when she told him that as long as her boys were there, she wouldn't share a room with him. It wasn't right.

She knew soon she'd need to call Chris in, drive him to school before going into work.

She stood at the kitchen sink, dressed in a tan-colored suit as she rinsed the breakfast dishes. As she bent over to start loading the dishwasher, she was startled when a hand suddenly smacked her backside. She shot up, whirled around and met Stone's grinning visage.

"You scared the daylights out of me, Stone Mitchell!"

He took her in his arms, and she grasped his forearms, smiling when he tucked her hair behind her ear and kissed it.

"I've got the boys working with my hands five miles to the north on a fence. The way I figure it, we've got plenty of time."

She arched away from him. "For what?"

"For me to have my wicked way with you," he growled.

Gina chuckled and pulled out of his arms. "You've been having that for a few days now. Sorry. I'm late for work. And you have to get Jack to school as I do with Chris."

She shut the door to the dishwasher and then washed her hands at the sink. He held out a towel and she took it and dried her hands, growing uncomfortable by his silence and the scowl on his face.

"I'll see you around five-thirty." She grabbed her purse off a kitchen chair and headed for the doorway. She'd hardly opened the door when it was slammed shut in her face. She whirled around, surprised to see Stone, crowding her back against the door.

His chest pressed against her, pinning her there and he ducked his head and brushed his beard against her forehead. Heat emanated from his body. "You don't need to go to work yet. After all, it's your own business. Just call Ruby and tell her you'll be late. Heck, better yet, why make a two-and-a-half-hour drive? Just tell her you're taking the day off."

It took a moment for Stone's words to register in Gina's mind. It was deplorable how he tempted her with his big, strong body, and when he kissed her lips, she forgot his words. Until he raised his head, took her hand, and tugged her with him down the hallway.

Gathering her wits she came to a skidding halt and pulled her hand from his. She glared at him and tapped her foot. "What do you think you're doing?" she said.

He raked a hand through his hair. "I must be losing my touch if you have to ask."

"You're trying to seduce me."

"Damned straight." His eyes were warm and possessive. "All

you need to do is cooperate. And don't think. Thinking always seems to pose problems for us."

When he reached out to take her hand again, she put it behind her back and moved away from him, shaking her head.

"You think what I do isn't important."

"Not true," he said impatiently. "It's just that I can take care of you. Hell, you got bills? Fork them over. There's no need for you to work so much."

Gina saw red. "You haven't heard a word of what I've been saying over the weekend, have you?"

He gave her a puzzled look. "Jeez, what's this all about?"

"Didn't I say I don't need a man making my decisions for me? And didn't you say you'd respect my wishes?"

"I do!" he retorted. "What does wanting to make love to you have to do with your work? Hell, I've just offered to help you out financially, freeing you up to spend more time with me, relax more, too, which would benefit both of us."

———

Gina gasped, "You are the most egotistical man I've ever met! I've clients, one each hour on the hour, today, beginning at ten. You think I should leave them high and dry just to romp with you in bed? I don't have time to get Chris to school today so I'll call him in that he's out for the day. I'll do the same with Jack since he'll gripe if we make him go to school when Chris isn't. But only today."

He opened his mouth then closed it, looking thoughtful. He frowned. "Maybe you're right. Maybe I'm more of a chauvinist than I realized."

"I don't need a father or another husband to think for me. My work is every bit as important to me as this ranch is to you."

Gina snatched up her briefcase from the floor and yanked open the door. Stone's hand closed around her wrist.

She glanced over her shoulder and saw confusion in his face. "I made a mistake. I'm sorry."

Gina shook her head, pulled her arm away. "You sure as hell did, cowboy."

She stalked away. Once she reached her car, she breathed a sigh of relief when she noticed he hadn't followed her. But he stood in the doorway, arms akimbo and legs spread, his face dark and angry, and confused.

She sped away furious with him for trying to do the very same thing Charlie had done throughout their marriage. But she was no malleable seventeen-year-old any longer. She wouldn't allow him to rule her and make decisions for her, especially ones she didn't agree with. Yet, she knew she wouldn't run out on him. Not again. She needed to try and work things out. While she hadn't agreed to marry him, they'd made a silent commitment to each other with their act of love. She sighed. Tonight they'd have to have another talk.

———

His argument with Gina put Stone in a melancholy mood, but it didn't take long for Jack and Chris to pull him out of it. He enjoyed the rest of the day with the boys, even if the temperature had risen to a hundred degrees. Usually, he retired inside his air-conditioned house by mid-afternoon, but he knew, with Gina leaving this evening after work, he wouldn't have much more time to spend with Chris.

Now he sat on a corral fence, his attention on Chris, who was maneuvering his horse around the ring. He'd gained more confidence since the first time he'd sat a horse. Still Jack, sitting beside him, complained about his younger brother.

"He's doing better, Jack," Stone said. "Ease up on him, will you?"

"He's too stiff in the saddle. He needs to loosen up," Jack

grumbled.

Stone gave Jack a gentle shove and he fell off the fence and landed on his feet inside the corral. "You were the same way your first few times out."

Which was an outright fib. Stone well recalled Jack's first time on a horse. He'd been a natural.

Stone watched Jack wander to his brother's side and give him a few pointers. He thought about Gina's anger this morning when she'd left the house for work, knowing she'd had good reason to be angry. He could kick himself for his insensitivity toward her and her work. But, damn! He knew several women who'd jump at the chance he offered. Having a guy love them, pay the bills, take care of them—just as he'd taken care of his mother all those years. What was wrong with that? Of course, Gina wasn't sick in the head the way his mother was, so he knew she'd do the household chores...wasn't that what housewives did, after all?

But then he thought Gina was her own boss, with her own business; he guessed she'd set up her hours with as many clients as she wanted so she still had time for her boys. She'd have time for him too, he decided. They could make this work. He'd hire a housekeeper and keep Marguerite on to cook.

He glanced at his watch and groaned as he dropped down from the fence. "Time to go in, boys. I want to get those burgers on the grill before your mom arrives."

"I'll just help Chris cool Rusty down," Jack said.

"Not too long," Stone warned. "We all agreed we'd do this cooking thing together."

"Heck, Stone," Jack grumbled. "*You* decided for us."

True. Stone grinned as he strode toward the house, then groaned at the prospect of grilling. He'd put in a long workday, and the very last thing he felt like doing was cooking supper.

Marguerite couldn't return soon enough from her vacation visiting friends and family in Mexico.

Just as he pulled a package of rock-hard beef patties from the freezer, placed it on a plate and shoved it in the microwave to defrost, he heard a car in the driveway.

He peered out the window to find Gina leaving her car. She'd removed her lightweight blazer and wore a sleeveless white top. He took in her lush hips and flat stomach in the narrow tan slacks and sighed.

He'd thought about her compact, pretty body off and on through the day while working, but his thoughts just didn't do justice to the real thing.

Gina came through the back door with Jack and Chris on her heels, each carrying a brown bag.

She moved aside to allow them through, her hesitant eyes on Stone. "Hi," she said softly.

He smiled. "Hi, yourself. Hard day?"

At the cupboard she proceeded to pull down plates to set the table. "Uh-huh, and then some. I've this new client and he, well, he sort of reminds me of you in some ways."

He frowned. *A new guy?*

CHAPTER SIXTEEN

He didn't like the sound of that. She chattered away, telling him all about the man. When he heard the word, 'cowboy', and tall and handsome, he saw red.

"What the hell are you doing, Gina?" he growled.

Three heads turned his way. Three pair of startled eyes stared at him.

"Excuse me?" Gina said.

What he'd wanted to ask was why she was having anything to do with another cowboy, when she had him. Instead, he said, "I haven't cooked the burgers so you don't have to rush to set the table," he muttered when all he wanted to do is interrogate her about this new guy.

She laughed. "Guess you didn't notice I brought home Chinese."

"Great," he murmured, then turned and put the plate of burgers in the refrigerator. They'll still be good tomorrow. "Didn't feel like cooking anyway." He strode from the kitchen, feeling eyes on him again. He called out, "I'll be right back."

Once he cleaned up and combed his hair, he stared at his

reflection in the mirror. *Get a grip, buddy. The guy's a client, nothing more.*

After supper, Stone said, "How about a ride?"

Jack and Chris rose from their chairs and whooped, "Yes!" They started to run from the kitchen, but Stone stopped them with his next order.

"We'll all stay and clean up first."

"Washing dishes is for sissies," Jack grumbled, returning to his chair. He slumped down and scowled at Stone.

Stone leaned forward, his elbows on the table. "Let me tell you something, son, I've never been married, and my mom worked long hours raising me. I've done plenty of dishes in my time. Do I seem like a sissy to you?"

"But you've got Marguerite now," Jack replied.

"True. But you know she's on vacation for the next month. No riding until the table has been cleared and dishes loaded in the dishwasher."

He came to his feet, snatched up his plate and rubbed elbows with Gina at the sink as she stood rinsing off dishes and stacking them in the dishwasher.

The boys grumbled but helped. Ten minutes later the three of them headed out to the barn to saddle their horses. Stone had wanted Gina to come but completely understood when she said she was tired.

Later that evening, Stone met up with Gina in the family room after the boys retired for the night. It hadn't taken much to convince her to stay another night. She was exhausted from her long workday, and it didn't help the commute was so long, which was a good thing for Stone.

"I owe you an apology," he said, settling beside her on the sofa.

"I owe you one," she replied.

He arched his brow. "What for?"

"For threatening to run out on you instead of trying to work things out."

He took her hand. "Never will I belittle your work, I promise. Didn't even realize I was doing it at the time. After you left, I thought about it a lot and realize I was."

"Thank you," she said softly. "But I think it's only fair I tell you this will be the last night I stay overnight. I need time to think about us, and I think Jack would fare better if I weren't here all the time."

"Jack's doing great, no need to worry about him." He frowned. "I don't have to think about us, Gina. I know you're my woman... the right woman for me."

She smiled. "Good. Chris and I will come out and spend weekends if that's still all right."

He heaved a sigh. "Weekends aren't enough, but it'll have to be for now."

———

Autumn sped by and winter arrived, along with the holiday preparations.

Gina and Chris never missed a weekend going to the ranch to visit Jack and Stone, and they'd been getting along great, even though Stone wasn't enamored of the once a week routine. Every weekend he griped about it—but never tried to sway her into staying. She couldn't blame him for he had his heart set on her she knew.

Gina had invited Stone to her house for a traditional Thanksgiving dinner. She and Chris had just finished making the gravy and setting the table when she heard the door burst open.

"Hey, Mom, bro," Jack said as he strolled into the kitchen, hands shoved deep into his jeans pockets. "How's it going?"

Gina grinned, thinking how cool, how grown up he sounded, likely jazzing it up to impress his younger brother. But when he stopped dead in front of her and smacked her cheek with a sloppy, wet kiss, she nearly keeled over in surprise.

"Happy Thanksgiving!" he exclaimed.

"You too, honey," she replied as tears filled her eyes.

She turned to find Stone leaning against the doorjamb, looking handsome with a new haircut and his beard very short and neatly trimmed. "I don't believe it. You paid Timothy another visit, didn't you?"

He nodded.

"Thought you said you were going to go to a straight barber."

He shrugged. "What can I say? The guy's got the talent and good taste. And we're used to each other now."

Gina chuckled when she thought about Timothy and the first time he 'came on' to Stone. "Well, you two are right on time," she said as she reached back to untie her apron.

Her eyes widened on Stone when he stepped up, placed his hands on her shoulders and spun her about, her back to him. Easily, he untied her apron and hung it from a hook near the oven.

"Thanks," she said softly. Lord, but he was handsome, and gentle, and kind, and sweet—and everything she should want in a man. So, why was she so hesitant to go the whole mile with him?

His glittering eyes seemed to be asking the same question when he spun around and headed for the turkey sitting on a cutting board on the countertop. He picked up the electric knife and proceeded to neatly cut up the turkey. She was envious. Whenever she had to do the chore, she'd hack the poor bird to pieces, but not Stone.

She couldn't believe it, but the four of them had nearly polished off a fourteen-pound turkey and all the trimmings. Conversation was lively and lots of laughter ensued. After they ate, they made fast work of cleaning up the kitchen since there was a football game on television they all wanted to watch. The boys were already situated in the living room, television blaring by the time Gina and Stone were ready to join them. Gina started out the door but stopped when Stone said, "Wait a minute."

She glanced at him over her shoulder and saw the curiosity on his face. "What?" Her eyes swept the kitchen. "We're all done now.

Besides, don't you want to see the cowboys beat those purple-people eaters again?"

Stone shook his head. "I'd like us to talk," he said quietly. A nervous prickle went up her spine and she clenched her hands together. Whenever Stone started thinking, which led to talking, it meant he had something of importance on his mind. Maybe he planned on asking her to marry him again. How many times had he done so, thus far? Twice, for certain.

Those initial nervous prickles turned to ones of delight now. For the first time she was beginning to think she could marry this guy who'd saved her elder son from destroying himself. Yet, deep down, she knew that wasn't reason enough.

During the past weeks she felt she'd done the right thing keeping away from Jack at the ranch during the week, and seeing him only on weekends, even though she missed him. Even Chris seemed at loose ends with his brother gone. But she couldn't deny Jack's disposition had improved, in large part because he truly liked Stone. He'd bonded with him and looked upon him as the father figure he needed in his young life.

She more than liked him.

She smiled when she thought of how Stone would tell her he loved her, just before she hung up the phone after speaking to him each night. It took a lot of courage for a man to say those three words, because love meant commitment. Stone was eager and ready to be married. Gina still wasn't certain. The big question was, could Stone allow her to maintain her cherished freedom if they married?

Stone took her arm and guided her down the hallway, toward her bedroom, instead of moving into the living room. She frowned as she looked into his pensive face. *Oh, Lord, don't tell me Jack's been caught in trouble again!*

In her bedroom he pressed her down on the side of the bed and he sat beside her. He didn't touch her but clasped his hands between his knees and stared down at the carpeting.

After a while, she grew nervous. "Stone? What is it? Is it Jack? What's he done now? You can tell me. Don't feel bad if he got out of hand and you couldn't control him, and…"

He raised his brow as he stood up. "He wouldn't dare," he growled. "Besides, he loves the ranch and wouldn't jeopardize his place here by getting into trouble. Jack's doing great."

Gina heaved a relieved sigh as she watched him pace the floor. "Then what's up?"

He stopped in his tracks. "How come you didn't invite your folks and family here for Thanksgiving? Or, how come you didn't go home for the holiday?"

Gina's spine stiffened. "How do you even know I have family?"

"Jack said you do."

"On his father's side, they're all deceased. On mine, yes, I have family—parents, and sisters, but I'm not on speaking terms with them."

"Since when?"

"Since before Jack was born fifteen years ago."

Stone's jaw dropped. "You've kept the boys from your family all this time?"

Gina heard the shock and surprise in Stone's voice. She grew defensive, thinking he had no idea how her father had treated her after learning she was pregnant, forcing her to marry Charlie, even though they hadn't been in love. Once she and Charlie married, they left Chicago, choosing Seattle, Washington as their new home, far away from her family. Gina had returned only a few times in the past years, to see her sisters and their families, but only on very special occasions.

She saw her mother once a year, during the summer, in Chicago, where they'd tour the town, see a play, and go out to dinner, leaving the boys behind with Charlie. And in the fall her mom would come out for a week to be with her and the boys. But she hadn't set eyes on her father nor spoken to him since her wedding day, even though her mother insisted he'd like to see her and meet his grandsons.

In a way, guilt plagued her over this but resentment toward her controlling father ran deep—she'd never forgive him and his dictatorial ruling in their home, not to mention his unsympathetic reaction when he learned she was pregnant. He'd made her feel like a worthless tramp. It had taken her years to get over her anger with him. Now she felt just dead, numb to him.

"My sons are my business. My familial relationships are my own. You worry about your family and I'll worry about mine. Where's your family, by the way."

"Never knew my father and Mom passed away a few years ago."

"Sorry," she murmured. "I recall you telling me that. No siblings?"

"Nope." He raked his hand through his hair and asked, "How can you have a guilt-free conscience over this? The boys told me they've never even met their grandfather. Call your dad, Gina."

"Over my dead body! If he wants to see us, he's the one who has to make the first move, not me."

"So, you're saying if he called you, came to see you, you wouldn't toss him out?"

She shrugged. "Maybe I would, maybe I wouldn't. All I know is he's never tried. Now, let's leave this alone. Don't ruin our holiday," she begged.

"Okay," he said slowly, "but I got to tell you something. If I had a family to call on, I'd have done it today. Don't waste any more precious time over past grievances because, in the end, does it really matter? And in the end, you'll regret it."

———

A week later, Gina sat in her office, recalling their argument on Thanksgiving, her conscience prickling her. Maybe it *was* time to bury the hatchet between herself and her father. She admitted they were too much alike—both stubborn, that's for certain!

She heard a door open and looked up to find Ruby standing in front of her desk, coat on, ready to leave for the day.

"I thought I'd work another hour or so," Gina said.

"Not on a Friday night, you're not. Besides, you've got to get me home in time for my date."

"Who is it this time?"

Ruby smiled dreamily. "Remember that tall, blonde chemical engineer I met at the Red Rooster Saloon a few weeks back during Karaoke hour?"

"You mean the guy who looks like a fair-haired Jerry Lewis in the Absent-Minded Professor?"

"Are you insinuating Robert is a nerd?"

Gina shrugged. "He's just not your usual type."

"You're right about that." Ruby sighed. "But for some reason I like him, and he likes me. What's funny is I've never gone for fair-haired, conservative-type guys with glasses until now."

"Why are you attracted to him?"

"That's personal."

Gina stared at her secretary in surprise then gasped when Ruby's cheeks turned pink.

"I don't believe it!" Gina crowed. "You mean to tell me you've gone to bed with him already?"

"It wasn't all that soon. We'd gone on three dates by then."

Gina sank lower in her chair and folded her hands under her chin, her eyes riveted on Ruby.

"Are you going to tell me about it?"

"No," Ruby said quickly. "I told you, it's none of your business."

Gina was quite frankly amazed by Ruby's reply since she normally bragged about her conquests.

"You really do like this guy, don't you?"

"Yeah," Ruby said, a slow grin brightening her face.

"I'm happy for you," Gina said sincerely.

"Thanks. Now let's get out of here. Robert is picking me up at seven." She tilted her head and frowned at Gina. "You know, you look a bit down. Everything okay out at the OK Corral?"

Gina smiled wryly. "Very funny."

Ruby shrugged. "Sorry. I have a hard time remembering the name of the place."

"It's Falcon's Ridge. And things are just fine. Jack is so happy on the ranch. He hasn't been involved with drugs or alcohol and he's given up the girlfriend, which makes me very happy. Now if I could only get over my fears of commitment, maybe Stone and I could make a life together."

They walked to the door. Ruby said, "It's easy to see, from what you've said, that you're the only one he wants to two-step with."

Gina nodded as she stepped in the hallway, turned, and locked the door, pocketing her keys. "True. But, I'm not sure if I want to marry a man so much like my father. He proposed to me, Ruby."

Horror crossed Ruby's face as they waited for the elevator to take them to the parking garage. "Proposed? You mean like—marriage? My Lord, what do you want to marry him for?"

"Because that's what people usually do when they fall in love. No need to worry, though, I told him I need more time. And I do." Gina locked the door.

"There's more to a relationship than marriage, you know," Ruby said.

"Let me guess," Gina said dryly. "You're telling me this due to your own vast knowledge of the institution, aren't you?"

A sad expression crossed Ruby's face and Gina was instantly contrite. "Oh, Ruby, I'm sorry. I don't mean to be so nasty."

The elevator doors opened, and Ruby stepped out and walked ahead of Gina toward her car.

"You're right," Ruby said. "I shouldn't be dealing out advice when I've struck out twice. But then, that's precisely why I don't want you leaping into marriage and making the same mistakes I did. You've told me about the highs and lows of your marriage to Charlie, and you stuck with him through it all. I guess I don't have as much tolerance as you do."

"I have no idea what to do, Ruby. I'm coming closer every day to saying yes, but like I said, he's holding out on me. I can tell."

Ruby followed Gina, pausing beside her car. "Why don't you just ask him?"

She gave Ruby a thoughtful look as she opened her door. "I just may. He's the one always badgering me about having heart to heart talks, and they're usually one-sided with me spilling my guts. It's about time he came clean with me."

"Maybe he's got financial problems and is afraid to tell you." Ruby shook her head as she sank down in the passenger seat. As she donned her seatbelt, she added, "No, that's not possible. Why in the world would he want to marry you when you're poor? Nope. Lack of money isn't his problem."

"Ruby," Gina said in exasperation as she buckled her own seatbelt. "I haven't checked out his bank account, if that's what you mean."

"That's okay. He owns his own spread so he's likely doing just fine. Whether you decide to marry him or not, I'd hang onto him. Like my mama always said: It's just as easy to fall in love with a rich guy as it is with a poor one."

"You are so practical it's frightening. And so utterly unromantic! I know I have to do something soon, though. I'm worried about Jack and Chris getting their hopes up about us marrying."

"What? Do you think your kids have been wearing blinders? I'll clue you in to something; they know more than we ever did at that age, believe me. It's a whole new generation out there now. My advice to you is to sit right down and be straight with them about you and Stone. Tell them you believe you're in love with him."

"I can't do that." Gina pulled onto the street and headed for home. "They'll expect us to get married. You know how much they'd enjoy having a new daddy. And they'd welcome Stone because they're crazy about him. But I'm not willing to take a chance and get their hopes up. If things don't work out between us it'll break their hearts. Besides, we truly haven't known each other long enough to make that kind of commitment to each other."

"Seems Stone doesn't think that way."

Gina shrugged. "He's been lonely, and admitted it to me, vowing to be married and settled down by Christmas. Told me that from the beginning."

Ruby said, "I remember you telling me that, but mark my words that you'll be making the biggest mistake of your life if you let that man get away. Just let me know when the coast is clear."

Gina gave her secretary a quick look. "Over my dead body."

Ruby chuckled. "Thought that would get a rise out of you. Home, Ms. Liberatti."

"I can't wait until your car is fixed."

CHAPTER SEVENTEEN

Gina managed to finish her holiday shopping two weeks before Christmas. She'd just entered her house with packages in both hands when Stone appeared in the hallway to help her. Stone had offered to come out to the house to keep an eye on Chris while she shopped. It was a lot easier for him to come in with Jack then for her to bring Chris down to the ranch, which was in the opposite direction of downtown.

She also told him she'd be home late and suggested he spend the night in her guestroom. He'd been happy to do so.

"Where are Jack and Chris?" she asked, setting the plastic bags on the table.

"In bed."

Gina arched her brow and shrugged out of her jacket. "So early?"

Stone scowled, took her jacket, and hung it on the back of the chair. "Have you any idea of the time?"

"Somewhere around nine, isn't it?"

"How about ten-thirty?"

"Oh!" She grinned and peered into a bag. "Guess I lost track of time. By the way, wait until you see what I found for Chris. He's going to love it!"

"Gina. Next time you're out late will you check in with me?"

Gina gave him a surprised look, stunned by the cool tone of his voice. "I told you this morning I was going shopping after work, which is why I had you come out here to meet Chris after school."

"I happen to know your last appointment was at two. I find it hard to believe you've been shopping all this time."

"You checked up on me?" she asked incredulously.

A defensive tone entered his voice. "I only called your office to get an estimate as to when you'd be home since I was cooking supper."

"I told you I likely wouldn't be home for supper. Darn it, Stone. You spoke to Ruby."

"No. Your office's cleaning lady answered, told me you'd left with Ruby earlier."

She glared at him before turning back to her purchases but didn't say another word.

The kitchen seemed unnaturally quiet to Gina as she examined the fringed suede jacket she'd purchased for Jack, an item he'd been begging for the past two years. She'd fully expected Stone to offer an apology by now, so she looked over her shoulder and was surprised to find he'd left the kitchen.

Gina shoved the jacket back inside the large bag, snatched up all her purchases and stuffed them inside the laundry room. She walked down the hallway and into the family room, then sat down on the sofa, threw her legs up on the coffee table and turned on the TV. Obviously, Stone had already gone to bed. This was the first time he'd be sleeping over at her place. The boys were bunked together in Chris' room, leaving Jack's room for Stone.

She needed to unwind and think.

After half an hour of flipping channels Gina heard footsteps in the hallway. When she turned she saw Stone enter the kitchen. Her eyes stayed riveted on his naked back, then traversed the length of it past his nicely shaped butt and long legs encased in blue jeans. She followed him into the kitchen and leaned against the doorjamb.

"Can't sleep?" she said.

Stone had his head buried in the refrigerator, but Gina heard his muffled words, "What do you think?"

Oh! He was in a mood.

He slammed the refrigerator door and clutched sandwich makings in his hands.

Gina sighed, wondering what in the world was wrong.

"Want one?" he asked just as she'd turned away, deciding he apparently wasn't interested in conversation.

She looked at him over her shoulder. "No, thanks." She stared at him awhile longer and asked, "Are you feeling okay?"

He nodded. "Fine." He slapped ham and cheese on bread, spread with mayonnaise, and a hunk of lettuce.

"I see." She cocked her head to one side and the longer she looked at him the more she could see he was angry with her and trying to maintain his distance, and his cool. "You're mad at me yet, aren't you?"

He shot her a quick glance, then took another bite of his sandwich, finishing off one half of it. He sank back in his seat and sprawled his long legs out to the side, crossing them at the ankles.

"I'm going to tell you about me, something that will help you understand why I'd like a phone call from you in future when you'll be out so late. Okay?"

"Okay," she said softly, sinking down in a chair at the table.

"I am assuming you had your cell with you."

She nodded and he continued.

"How long have we known each other, Gina?" he finally asked.

She looked at him, confused. "You know the answer to that. Nearly six months, I believe."

"Would you say that's a long time?"

"Chronologically, no."

He pierced her with a discomfiting look. "Do you believe in that short time we've learned to know each other well?"

"Yes, I think so," she said.

"I disagree. Sometimes I feel I know you real well. Other times I don't. You allow me to see surface things about yourself, but nothing deep."

She came to her feet. "You know what? I've been feeling the same thing about you. You're holding something back from me while I've been straightforward and honest with you. I've told you countless things about myself, including about my aversion to marriage—losing control of my life."

Stone rose and leaned across the table. "Listen, sweetheart. Six months may not be all that long, but I know that I'm in love with you. You obviously don't feel as strongly about me. Do you have any idea how that makes me feel?"

She saw that his face had paled and that he'd clenched his fists, yet his body shook like the last leaves of autumn clinging to their branches.

"I'm growing tired of waiting for you to make up your mind," he said softly.

"Wait! Why are you avoiding my question? Tell me about your past, Stone."

He'd risen from his chair and stared at her.

"What happened when you were a ranger? Marguerite said to ask you about it. I'm doing it now. I've a feeling it will make a difference between us if I knew why you left the force. You said you'd gotten into some sort of brawl and your face had been scarred."

Gina could see it was difficult for him to reply, but he did. She heard him sigh deeply and watched him lean against the pantry door, arms folded.

"I told her I'd tell you, and I will, now. I joined the rangers straight out of law enforcement school. It was difficult work, Gina, dangerous work." He sighed. "I'd been a caretaker to my mom all those years, so it seemed to make sense that once she died, I'd be watching out for others so going into law enforcement made sense, at the time.

"I worked as a ranger for four years and had had a long string of good luck, until I met up with the one bad guy I couldn't handle. He knifed me," he said haltingly, "real bad." He raised a hand and slid it down one side of his hairline, from temple to chin. "Then he left me for dead when he stabbed me in the gut. They found me lying in a pool of blood. They weren't sure I was going to make it. I was lucky."

"So, that's why you've an aversion to shaving," Gina replied dully. "When you said you had some scars, I figured it was no big deal. Apparently, I was wrong." She raised her eyes to his, trying to school the sadness in her eyes and in her heart.

She hadn't succeeded because he snarled, "Don't pity me, Gina, for crissakes."

"It's impossible not to. You're lucky to be alive. But the scars don't change who you are. You are a decent, honest, hard-working man. Why were you keeping this such a big dark secret?"

He shrugged. "I planned on telling you soon." A slow grin settled over his visage. "Now that you know, there's no reason why we can't set a date, is there? I mean if that's all that's been holding you back."

"I need more time."

Disappointment crossed his face. "Not much more can I give you, sweetheart," he said softly. "The rest of my life I've been honest with you." But then he smiled as he snaked an arm around her waist and kissed her until she felt woozy. When he finally lifted his head, he said, "You know where I live, sweetheart. But what are you going to do next time you're out late?"

"I promise I'll call you."

A week later Stone sat slumped on his sofa, going through big-time withdrawal from Gina. He hadn't seen her at all since he'd told her about his scars. And he'd done the most impetuous thing ever—he'd shaved. He admitted he'd astonished himself when he finished the job and stared in the mirror, hardly recognizing himself. The puckered scars had shrunk somewhat, had healed well and weren't as obvious as he'd remembered them to be.

Yet, he worried that the prospect of Gina seeing him clean-shaven wasn't something she could handle. He'd called her once a night during the week, but she'd either been Christmas shopping or working late Chris said. He'd looked forward to seeing her over the weekend, but Chris had come down with the flu and had been sick the entire weekend.

He'd been thinking a lot about his childhood and adolescent years growing up with no father, and a mom who worked all the time. Then he thought how he'd cared for his mom during his later teen years and into his twenties, when she'd come down with cancer. How protective he'd been, how he thrived on being in charge.

He thought about his life as a Texas Ranger, a job he'd easily given up to go into ranching. He pondered his current occupation as a rancher, a life he'd dreamed of since adolescence, and a fierce contentment stole over him.

Finally, he thought about all the human beings he'd known in life. Most had been women, and the few men hadn't been the type a young man would want to emulate. Maybe, if he'd seen the love between a man and a woman, his mom, and his dad, for example, he'd know what was holding Gina back from loving him and making a commitment.

Damn, but he had to convince Gina to marry him. Marguerite's words entered his mind then. Just little things she'd said over the past three years about finding himself a lady. One he could romance, woo and eventually marry.

He sat up straight on the sofa. That was it. Gina needed to be romanced. He'd planned on doing exactly that a few months back, until Jack got into trouble. Then he'd had easy access to Gina when she visited her son, but he'd never really courted a woman before and tried to decide what she'd like. He figured she'd enjoy the standard presents such as flowers, candy, and maybe even some pretty lingerie.

He'd start right away tomorrow morning. He folded his hands at the back of his head and leaned against the sofa, grinning at the prospect of courting Gina.

———

"I don't want to get a Christmas tree today or tomorrow. I don't think we should get one at all."

Gina stood at the sink frowning at Chris who sat at the kitchen table hunched over his bowl of cereal. It was nine o'clock Saturday morning, a week before Christmas and they still hadn't purchased a tree.

Chris had been completely unmanageable lately; in her book he needed a major attitude change. She'd been forced to ground him and now she was paying the price for it but knew she couldn't back down. Unfortunately, his whining was nearly driving her insane.

Probably withdrawal symptoms from not seeing Stone and Jack, she guessed. With Jack and Stone living at the ranch, things were pretty quiet around her house, though they'd regularly visited on weekends, this weekend no. It was time to pick out a tree and set it up.

She smiled as she thought about Stone's thoughtfulness over the past week. He'd sent her a dozen long-stemmed red roses one day; an enormous box of gold-foil wrapped chocolate candies the next. A few days passed without any gifts, but then with the next day she opened a prettily wrapped box to find a pair of pink-thong underwear. Just the thought of wearing them made her blush; just the thought he'd given them to her made her shiver in delight.

This courting side of Stone was something she hadn't seen before, but she loved it. Unfortunately, Stone seemed to be as strong-willed as Charlie had been but was proving to be more adaptable to change. Maybe there was hope for them.

"If Stone and Jack come, I'll go," Chris said slyly.

"Christopher," Gina chided. "That is the most ridiculous thing I ever heard. Stone has no interest in looking for a tree with us. And Jack is being punished for his crimes so he won't be coming home for Christmas. We'll go out to the ranch for the day. Stone already invited us."

"They *do* want to get a tree!"

Gina narrowed her eyes. "And how would you know that?"

"I talked to Stone yesterday."

"He called you?" she asked casually.

Chris shook his head and his complexion reddened. "Stone was here when I got home from school."

Gina sighed. "What did I tell you about opening doors to people when I'm not home?"

"Stone's no stranger, Mom! Jack came, too. Stone took us to Wendy's for burgers."

No wonder Chris hadn't been hungry for supper last night.

"Besides," said Chris, tilting up his chin and giving her a defiant look. "Just 'cause you're mad at Stone doesn't mean we should be, does it?"

Leave it to a twelve-year-old to put her in her place.

She sighed. "I'm not mad at him." *Just being cautious.* "Call him if you want, but if he isn't available today, I'm sorry. We've waited long enough to get a tree and this is the only day I can do it."

"Thanks, Mom!"

While she loaded the dishwasher she listened in on Chris's call to Stone—short, sweet, and excited. When he hung up the telephone and turned to her, his face was wreathed in a huge smile. "He said they'll be here in an hour."

She frowned. "You mean over two hours."

He shook his head. "Nope, they were on their way here before I called them!"

Gina was thoroughly disgusted with herself when she felt her heart flip-flop at the thought of seeing the blasted cowboy again.

And see him she did, in all his shaven glory.

She gasped and her hand flew to her mouth as he stood on her doorstep. He looked embarrassed, his tanned complexion flushed pink, chin tilted high as he meet her eyes. Then she shook her head and walked right into his arms. With tears in her eyes, she nuzzled his clean jaw and said, "I think I'll miss the softness of your beard."

He grinned. "No need to worry. I'm growing it back right away." He pushed her away from him, gently grasped her upper arms and said, "I just needed to show you."

Jack said, "I told him he should just get a cool-ass tattoo to cover it up."

Gina gasped. "No!"

They all laughed at her emphatic response. She examined his scar, amazed that he'd survived after what appeared to be a vicious knife attack. There was one long scar on the left side of his face that ran from his temple to beneath his jaw. It was pink and puckered. How painful it must have been, she mused.

She met his eyes and said candidly, "And for this little imperfection you grew that thick beard?" She touched the scar and added, "Does it hurt?"

"Not anymore." He took her hand and traced the length of the scar.

She thought how he'd bared himself to her, met his eyes and said with utter conviction, "You truly do love me."

Stone rolled his eyes. "It's about time you believed me. Now, the question is, can you live with me like this?"

She wound her arms around his neck and held on tight. After a moment she realized he hadn't reciprocated the embrace. She released her hold and stared at him as tears gathered in her eyes. "That scar is of no importance to me," she said softly. "The better question is can I live with your dictatorial ways?"

She didn't expect a reply and he didn't give her one, but just stared at her in silence.

———

Two hours later, Gina, her boys and Stone returned to the house with a tree, which he immediately plunked into the waiting stand.

"It's too big for our living room," Gina announced, giving the magnificent fir a critical look where it stood in a corner.

"It's perfect!" Jack said.

"It's the best tree we ever got!" Chris exclaimed.

Gina glanced at Stone who sat in the middle of her sofa, arms draped across the back.

"Thanks for helping us," she said. "There's no way I could have brought home a tree this size on my own."

Stone smiled faintly and shrugged. "No problem."

"I appreciate it." He looked so wonderful sitting there on her sofa; so *right*.

"Would you like to stay for supper?"

"You're not just asking just because of the boys, are you?"

Gina bristled. "I hate how you make me out to be the bad guy when I'm not." He gave her a skeptical look. "I'm not," she insisted. "Just because I haven't come to a decision…"

She bit her lip, turned away and stared blindly at the tree, her heart filled with sadness. Stone's hands settled on her shoulders and she sighed when he pulled her against him.

"Listen, Gina. I'm not the one who has a problem with commitment."

"I know," she muttered.

He released her and they headed down the hallway to the kitchen.

Stone stayed for supper, much to Chris's enthusiasm and delight. He'd missed his older brother.

Later, after the boys were in bed, Stone decided it was now or never that he tried winning Gina over. The flowers, candy and lingerie had softened her up he knew, but now he was on to bigger, more important things.

After supper, as they sat on the sofa in the family room, Stone said, "I want to show you something."

She raised her brows and watched him leave the house, only to return within moments with a large briefcase.

He set it down on her coffee table and unzipped it.

There were all kinds of colorful literature, flyers and brochures from various places of business—caterers, florists, formal wear shops. Her vision blurred when he started talking.

"Here's a calendar. Let's decide on a date. I'm willing to give up the idea of getting married by Christmas if you still need more time, but I'd like to start planning the wedding."

CHAPTER EIGHTEEN

S he was so astonished at first, she couldn't reply. After a long moment she said, "You've started planning our wedding? Before I've even consented?"

His eyes pierced hers. "All I've done is picked up brochures and information. You know you'll agree eventually. With time you'll see we're meant for each other. I love you and your kids. I can offer you so much, Gina."

"I can't believe you're doing this," she whispered, shaking her head as she stared at the brochures. "Especially since there's the possibility I'd turn you down, you know," she bristled.

He leaned over and feathered the tip of one of her ears with his lips. "You won't, will you?"

Gina saw the frown on his face, and the worry in his eyes and almost told him no, until she noticed a phone number on a brochure. She recognized the number then and looked him in the eye. "Have you been to see my church's priest?"

"Sure have," Stone said proudly. "He's making an exception for us about the marriage classes. Since we aren't spring chickens, he figures we should know what we're getting into so we don't have to take them."

She fisted her hands at her sides and narrowed her eyes. "You were that confident I'd say yes?"

He frowned. "I haven't planned the wedding. I just started gathering information. I thought you could do the actually deciding. I guess I was wrong thinking you'd love being surprised."

"Oh, I'm surprised all right, but you're right. I don't like it. I haven't decided if I want to be married again."

He leaned forward and folded his hands between his legs. "I thought if I started planning, you'd know that I'm serious about marrying you. That you'd take it as another sign of my love for you. It's the scar on my face. That's what's bothering you, isn't it? Rest assured I'll never shave these whiskers again, Gina."

"Oh, my God, it's not that at all," Gina whispered and in the next moment she was in his arms. She squeezed him and said, "It's your blasted stubbornness, and the fact you don't believe I can take care of myself when I can."

He released her and cupped her chin in one big hand. "Do you believe that I love you, with all my heart, with all my soul?"

"Yes," she said, her voice trembling.

"Then believe it'll work between us."

"I'll try." Through her tears she gave him a brilliant smile. "Okay?"

He looked at her suspiciously. "Okay, what?"

"I'll think about this—about us."

"You do that. Next time we talk I hope you'll say yes."

He was a good man and she had a feeling he'd spend the rest of his life trying to make her happy. She could think of far worse things in life than having a man love her with all his heart and soul. But first she had to be positive he wouldn't steamroll over her and make all the decisions in her life. How she'd figure that out she had no idea, but she had to try.

———

Gina's younger sister, Sofia, who lived a single life in Chicago, arrived unexpectedly on Christmas Eve, bearing gifts and glad tidings. They hadn't seen each other since last Christmas and were thrilled to be together again. Their older sister, Maria, also lived in Chicago with her husband and two children, near Gina's parents.

Maria had always been the dutiful daughter. She'd married a man of whom the family thoroughly approved, and they spent every Christmas in the welcoming embraces of the Liberatti family.

Gina would enjoy visiting her mother during the holidays but knew her father wouldn't accept and welcome her into the family home, even though, according to her mother, he said he would but was too proud to invite her.

"Can't you stay through the New Year?" Gina begged as she sat beside Sofia on the sofa, in front of the marvelous tree Stone had helped them decorate. To Gina it seemed as though they'd hardly finished cleaning up all the discarded gift wrap on the living room floor when Sofia announced she had to leave. Jack and Chris had said their goodnights a scant hour ago to game in their rooms; it seemed strange having Jack home for the holiday, but wonderful, too.

"I'd love to stay, but you know I can't. I'm scheduled to work a two-week hitch beginning tomorrow afternoon."

Gina frowned. "So, when do you have to leave?"

Sofia glanced at her watch. "My plane leaves in about an hour."

"What!" Gina exclaimed. "That soon?"

"Unfortunately, yes. I've already called a cab which should be here any moment."

"You purposely didn't tell me you were leaving so soon," Gina said, trying to conceal the hurt in her voice.

"You've got that right. You always give me so much grief about it. Besides, you know how I love my job."

"I'm happy for you," Gina said and sniffled. "How's your stomach, anyway?"

"Much better." Sofia chuckled. "You know, switching careers

made all the difference in the world. Besides suffering from that awful ulcer, I believe I would have eventually had a nervous breakdown."

Gina sighed. "You truly had no other option than to change jobs. It's a bonus that you're happy with your work, though."

Sofia had been a stockbroker with an esteemed house, and the job had nearly killed her. Once she'd been diagnosed with a bleeding ulcer a year ago, she'd changed jobs. She was an airline attendant now and not only did she enjoy the work it was easier on her nerves and she worked only fourteen days a month instead of twenty but was paid a full-time rate. And of course there was the advantage of seeing new places, too.

Shortly, Sofia's cab arrived, and the sisters hugged and gave each other a tearful farewell.

"Call me when you get back," Gina said as she carried her sister's suitcase to the cab.

Sofia pecked Gina's cheek. "I will." She settled into the cab, shut the door, and rolled the window down an inch. "Good luck with your cowboy. I'd like to meet him next time I visit."

"Sure." Gina smiled sadly as the cab sped away. She softly added, "Maybe, someday."

As Gina entered her house a lonely feeling settled over her. She poured herself another glass of champagne and sat down on the sofa. As she thought about her sisters and the rest of her family, she pondered the idea of trying to make amends with her father, but after a moment set the idea to rest. She'd inherited her stubborn streak from him, and she had a hunch she'd need to do a lot of groveling to get back into his good graces. Which she wasn't ready to do quite yet—if ever.

Later, she was on the ragged edge of sleep on her couch when the doorbell's peeling ring roused her. Jack beat her to the door.

"Didn't you hear the bell, Mom? It must have rung five times," he grumbled. Jack reached out and yanked open the door.

Gina snatched up her glass of champagne and looked at Stone standing in her foyer, clad in a leather suit. *The* leather suit.

Oh, my heavens. Marguerite had been right. She devoured his magnificent physique in the black, welt-seamed jacket he wore over a crisp white shirt and bright red Christmas tie. Her eyes drifted down over his sinewy thighs in narrow black leather pants.

Jack's complaining caught her attention then.

"If you two are going to just stand there and gawk at each other, fine. I'm going back to bed."

Gina chuckled and Stone laughed outright at Jack as he stumbled away down the hallway.

"Merry Christmas," Stone said, his low voice filled with amusement.

"You too," said Gina. "Here, let me take your jacket."

Stone glanced at the champagne she set down on a side table. "Company still here?"

She shook her head. "No. My sister left a while ago for the airport."

"Champagne?" he inquired.

"Hmm, yes. Would you like a glass?"

"You twisted my arm," he said with a grin.

Gina led him into the living room, and he sank into her sofa and stretched out his long legs. She moved to the bar in the corner of the room and her hand shook when she poured him a flute. She approached him, reached out and handed him his drink. Then she sat down in a chair across from him.

"Smells wonderful in here," Stone said. "Turkey?"

"Yes." She frowned. "You ate, didn't you?"

"Yes, but somehow Mexican food for Christmas doesn't quite make it. You know?"

Gina remembered Stone saying he'd be spending Christmas with Marguerite and her huge family, as he did every year. She asked, "Would you like me to fix you a plate?"

He rubbed his stomach. "That would be great."

Stone followed her into her kitchen. He sat down at the table while she pulled containers from the refrigerator.

"I like what you're wearing."

"Thanks." Her ankle-length red knit skirt and matching trendy vest over a white turtleneck was comfortable yet festive. She glanced at him over her shoulder. "I like your suit."

Oh, boy, did she like it. His potent masculinity made her legs go weak.

She dished up sliced turkey, dressing, green beans, mashed potatoes, and gravy and heated the plateful in the microwave. The buzzer rang and she pulled the plate out and set it down on the table in front of him.

Just as she turned away, he snatched her wrist and dragged her down to his lap. He held her there with one hand around her shoulders and the other across her abdomen. Then he captured her lips with his own in a deep, long kiss.

When he lifted his head she gazed into his dark smoldering eyes. She tried to stand but his hand settled on her rear and he held her in place.

"You aren't going anywhere until I get a Merry Christmas kiss," he drawled.

Gina narrowed her eyes. "I believe I just did."

"Nope. *I* kissed you."

She sat there and stared at him, her cheeks heating under his intent gaze.

"Guess you might need some inspiration," he drawled.

He dug inside his pocket and pulled out a sprig of mistletoe. He held it above his head, a silly grin on his lips.

She sighed. "Oh, well. I certainly don't want to be accused of not upholding tradition." She leaned down and gave him a scorching kiss. When she raised her head, she saw the dazed expression on his face. Quickly, she rose from his lap and nimbly danced away with a laugh when he growled and reached for her but missed. He settled back in his chair again. "Contrary to what you may believe, I didn't come all the way out here for a quick lay."

Gina's cheeks heated. "I know that."

He gave her an intimate smile. "I've a quick cure, you know. One that will allow us to enjoy each other every night for the rest of our lives."

"What are you saying?" she asked, moving back to his side. He'd suggested they marry before and she'd balked at the idea. Now she knew she wanted to marry him but first they'd have to set things straight between them. And she'd have to trust him to uphold their bargain once they were married.

She thought about how angry he'd been when she hadn't returned home from shopping until late. In hindsight, she realized she should have called and let him know she'd be late, especially since he'd had her boys. But that's precisely one of the reasons she hadn't called; it seemed in the past she'd always been accountable to some male in her life and she truly enjoyed not being accountable now. Who was she kidding? She was accountable to her sons and would be for quite a few more years. With a sigh she thought it wouldn't be so tough being accountable to Stone if he were reasonable about it and allowed her to be independent to work and live her life with him as equals.

"Check my right pocket."

She watched him carefully. He looked like a big cat waiting to pounce on his supper. Tentatively, she reached down, and she felt the square shape of a box.

"Go on, pull it out. It's your Christmas present."

Gina knew what it was, and she gasped even as tears welled in her eyes once more.

He groaned. "Don't you go cryin' on me."

She withdrew the black velvet box from his pocket while at the same time he snaked out an arm and drew her down to his lap again. Slowly, she opened the lid, peered inside, gasped, and closed it. "Oh, Stone," she breathed softly, clutching the small box to her chest.

"If you don't like it, we can always take it back for another."

"Over my dead body!" she announced and flipped open the lid again. Inside was the most exquisite set of rings Gina had ever seen. She widened her gaze on the platinum wedding band and engagement ring, set with a perfectly round diamond the size of her pinky in the center, with baguette diamonds on either side.

"We haven't discussed more children, but I'd like a couple more. How do you feel about that?"

"More children?" she squeaked.

She hadn't expected that, but she should have, she supposed. Heavens, her sons were half grown already, but she was only thirty-three... A warm feeling encompassed her then as she thought about having a baby with Stone. They had a lot to discuss before the wedding. Yes, they did, including her saying yes. She loved him.

She looked at Stone again and caught his shoulders shaking, noted a peculiar look on his face. When she saw the laughter lurking in his eyes, she shoved his shoulders and scowled.

"Don't you laugh at me, Stone Mitchell! This is a very important, serious moment in our lives."

He pulled her into his arms again, still perched on his knee. "Just say yes, damn it."

"You've got to ask me properly."

He dipped his head and kissed her breath away.

When he set her away from him again, she said, "It's very important to me that you ask properly." Gina felt heat steal into her cheeks, and she looked down at the ring. "You see, Charlie never did because my father *told* him he had to marry me."

Gina sat in abject silence on Stone's knee. He'd removed his hands from around her and she closed her eyes, dreading to look at the expression on his face, guessing he'd be humiliated by her demands. Could she blame him?

Suddenly, she found herself on her feet, Stone standing beside her as he shoved her down into the chair. She gasped and covered her mouth when he sank to one knee beside her. His voice was low, and his words touched her deeply, and were more than she'd ever hoped to hear.

"Marry me, Gina," he said, his low voice filled with love and warmth. "Be the love of my life. I can't live another day without you. I love you more than I thought it ever possible to love someone."

She nodded her head quickly and whispered, "Yes."

He kissed the knuckles on her left hand before turning it over and kissing her wrist, holding it all the while in his big, callused hand. "I've wanted a family of my own for a long time, my whole life, to be truthful. At first, I was uncertain whether I could make a life-long commitment to any woman, because of my father." He frowned and added, "Did I tell you I never knew him? I've never even seen a picture of him. Mitchell is my mother's name, so please, bear in mind, any children we have will have that name."

Gina saw the pain in his face as he spoke about the father he'd never known. She took his face in her hands and kissed him gently, then lifted her head and smiled. "It doesn't matter," she said softly. "It isn't important. This is where *we* begin, together, and a name doesn't mean a damned thing. I love you and you love me. That's all that matters."

He wound his arms around her, crushing her against him. After they'd moved into the living room, they sat surrounded by the warmth of Christmas night, before the twinkling lit evergreen. They spoke about their love for each other and they made plans about children, Stone finally agreeing that two together would be enough —four including her sons—their sons now, he stated firmly. And with the dawning of Christmas morning they moved down the hall together to seek their beds for a few hours rest.

Gina stopped at a door and opened it. Stone peered inside at what appeared to be a guest bedroom.

He drew her into his arms and whispered, "Now that we're getting married, it's not necessary we sleep apart, is it?"

She pressed against his shoulders and arched back from him. "I've two impressionable boys in the house, Stone. What a question?"

Immediately he released her. "Sorry." Then he swept his hand through his hair. "Truthfully, I forgot about them." He sighed and said, "Good-night, darling."

Gina didn't move but said, "I heard that sigh. What's wrong?"

He leaned one broad shoulder against the doorjamb and Gina sighed this time. Oh, how she wanted to step into that bedroom with him!

"I'd planned on being married by today." He lifted his head and stared at her in chagrin.

"We will be soon enough," she promised as she leaned into him, dipped her head back, inviting his kiss.

After the kiss he smiled and closed the door in her face. Gina stood there, struck speechless, unable to believe he'd given up so easily. But then a smile of satisfaction crossed her lips; he was learning.

———

Gina wakened from a deep sleep, to the sound of voices; several of them. And squeals of laughter, then hushes. She smiled. Her boys were awake. She turned, glanced at her bedside clock, and saw it was eight o'clock. Christmas morning had arrived. She smiled when she heard Stone's deep voice talking to the boys, followed by the sound of rattling pots and pans. Oh, my Lord, what were they up to now, she wondered?

Upon hearing the doorbell ringing and doors opening and shutting, and more voices, she sat up. Then she frowned when she decided they sounded remarkably like voices from her past.

"Regina Theresa! Where are you?" a voice suddenly shouted outside her door.

It was unbelievable, Gina thought. She could have sworn she heard her father shouting. He was the only one who called her Regina. The last time she'd seen Roberto Liberatti, her father, was well over two years ago when her sister Maria's eldest son, Thomas, had been confirmed. She'd left the boys home with Charlie and, even though she hadn't wanted to attend, she did so because Maria had begged her.

At that event she and her father had managed to successfully avoid each other. Even though they'd never seen eye to eye on most things, much to her father's disappointment, Gina, who'd always been his unsaid favorite, had also been the most rebellious.

While Maria, her older sister obeyed him explicitly, Sofia tended to ignore him and managed to keep a low profile. Gina had been the argumentative one, which was strange since she hardly ever argued with anyone else. Yet, she'd always stood up for herself and faced him down with her own differing opinions and beliefs.

Gina shot straight up in her bed when the bedroom door burst open and her father's robust body appeared in the doorway. She scrambled to her feet and stood on the opposite side of the bed from him, jamming her hands on her hips. Luckily, the night had been cool, and she'd worn her old flannel nightgown. The man still managed to make her feel like a kid as he stood there, a big toothy white grin on his face.

"Why are you barging into my bedroom this early in the morning, Father?" she snapped. *Come to think of it, why was he barging in at all? And the bigger question, what was he doing here?*

"Hmm," he said, tugging his red and gold paisley vest over his substantial paunch. "You used to call me Poppa. Why so formal now?"

"Maybe because we've been estranged for the past fifteen years has something to do with it."

His swarthy complexion reddened at her reply and he stared at her in silence, the room crackling with tension until Stone appeared.

He looked between the two of them. "What is this, a staring contest or something? I gather you two haven't made up yet."

Gina widened her eyes on Stone. "Do you mean to tell me you invited him here, to my home, and on Christmas?"

"Yes, I invited him." He glanced at his watch. "By the way, everyone's waiting for you to get dressed so we can open gifts."

"Why did you ask my father to come?"

"Right after you agreed to marry me, I called him. I explained that we were getting married soon and that I'd like to meet the family. He agreed."

Roberto cringed and looked at Stone. "Guess I forgot to mention that we haven't been on speaking terms for years."

Stone shrugged. "I knew and it doesn't matter. Get over it—the both of you."

Roberto looked hurt and embarrassed. Gina sighed. Her father could really turn it on when he wanted to. It all had to do with control, and he'd try and get it any way he could.

"I'll leave you two alone to discuss this situation, Stoney."

After he left Gina scowled at Stone. "Stoney?"

He shrugged. "I wasn't going to argue with your father, Gina. He can call me 'jackass' for all I care. I just want him to accept me."

She threw her hands up. "Here's another example of how you take charge and don't tell me a thing—don't include me in making decisions. And you expect us to get married? How could you? You have no idea how miserable that man made my life. I can guarantee you that I wouldn't have married Charlie if he hadn't forced me."

Stone was silent for a minute, a thoughtful expression on his face. Finally he said, "I'm convinced your dad did what he thought was best for you at the time." He sighed. "You were pretty young, after all. That, unfortunately, is what parents do. I mean, look at all that's happened with Jack? Do you regret calling on Tough Love for help? No, I don't think so, at least not right at this moment. But, in hindsight, you may later come to realize you made some mistakes along the way. Your father made a mistake, and you made some, too. But it's done and over with. Forgive him. He really wanted to see you and the boys, and the boys wanted to see him—meet him."

She fisted her hands at her side, hating the tears welling in her eyes. "It's not that easy!"

Gina stalked around the bed and stopped in front of him. "Did it never, ever occur to you that you should have asked me first to meet my family? Didn't you think eventually I would have introduced you to them? Even my father?"

"I figured eventually you would," Stone murmured as he sank onto the bed, leaned forward, and folded his hands between his legs. "I thought you'd be happy that I'd taken the initiative to do this. That you'd take it as another sign of my love for you. We can't discuss everything before coming to a decision, can we? Sometimes we just need to do it on our own."

"If it's something this important we most certainly must."

He sat there awhile in silence, staring down at his feet. Finally, he raised his gaze to hers. "I'm sorry, Gina. What else can I say?"

Gina clenched her hands at her sides as tears filled her eyes. "I just wished you hadn't done it. I don't want to think about marrying you right now." She swiveled on her heel and headed for the door.

Stone rose and started to follow her. "Where are you going?"

"Out."

"Where?"

She whirled around and jammed her fists on her hips. "Just out. I don't have to tell you or anyone else where I'm going, but I won't be gone long." She took a deep breath and added, "I'd like you to be gone before I return."

"What! Now wait a minute, Gina…"

"No, you wait a minute! From the moment we met you haven't really listened to me. I said I don't want some man dominating my life again—controlling what I do. I don't want to be accountable to you or any other man. Ever."

She turned the knob and yanked the door open, but his words froze her.

"Damn it, Gina. Everyone is accountable to somebody, at some time or another. Everybody!"

She glared at him over her shoulder and scoffed, "And who are you accountable to, Stone?"

He growled, "To the hands on my ranch, to Marguerite. To the county because of the kids I care for out at the ranch. To you and your boys if you'll let me. You see, it works both ways." He raked a shaky hand through his hair then met her eyes again. "Remember that night I was angry when you stayed out until ten?"

She nodded.

"All kinds of horrible thoughts ran through my mind, including the possibility of you being involved in a car accident, especially when I learned you'd left the office by two o'clock. Eight hours of shopping just didn't seem possible," he said dryly.

Stone walked toward her and stopped right in front of her. He wound an arm around her waist and drew her close. "It's Christmas," he murmured, "And I think it's time you were reunited with him. I wished I'd had a dad, Gina."

"Not one like mine." She pulled out of his arms and fled down the hallway. As she left, a niggling guilty sensation came over her at the realization that what he said made a lot of sense. But she was just too hurt and angry to see reason.

With a groan Stone leaned against the doorjamb until he heard the front door slam.

———

Gina was glad she'd snatched up her lightweight jacket when she left the house. Her cheeks heated at the astonished looks on her mother and sisters' faces as she stormed by them without a word, mostly because she figured they had to have heard some of hers and Stone's conversation.

She stared down at her feet as she walked down the sidewalk. Just as she turned the corner, she heard a familiar whistling and she looked up. Her father was slowly moving toward her, his big body covered in a heavy overcoat, one she knew was too warm for Texas and meant for Chicago winters. He hadn't noticed her yet and in that moment she realized she had inherited one of his traits; staring down at the sidewalk as she walked. Why hadn't she ever noticed that before?

He happened to look up, noticed her. He came to a stop, a wary expression on his face. Now that surprised her since he'd always been confident and secure in his beliefs, and never showed any signs of insecurity around her or anyone else.

With a deep sigh she moved toward him. It was now or never and definitely past time to bury the hatchet. She plastered a scowl on her face to conceal her own insecurity as she approached him. She stopped directly in front of him and deepened her scowl. "Father? Why are you wearing your overcoat when it's sixty-five degrees outside? And why aren't you inside with everyone else? You could have gotten lost."

He raised his brow. "Lost? Going around the block?" He shook his head. "As for my coat, well, it is winter, isn't it?"

Gina sighed. Leave it to her dad to have a reply. She saw sweat dripping down the sides of his face, and knew he'd never admit he was hot. It was December—winter—even if they were in southern Texas.

Gina braced herself as she waited for him to continue, guessing he'd harp on her about hers and Stone's argument. Therefore, she was amazed when he gave an elaborate shrug and merely said, "Needed some fresh air."

Gina's jaw gaped. Where was the lecture? Why hadn't he berated her or started in on hollering at her for not visiting the family in years, or a host of other faults he usually dumped on her? Faults that still, to this day, hurt beyond the pain of giving birth to two sons.

"It's good to see you, Gina. I've missed you."

Her jaw gaped further.

"Close your mouth, Cara Mia, then we'll find a nice quiet place to sit and talk. Something we should have done years ago."

Gina had no idea how to respond to that but when he took her arm and led her a few blocks away, she went with him, her body numb. They stopped at a park bench and sat side by side. Her local neighborhood park was quiet this late morning as folks were hustling about their holiday activities. After a long moment's silence Gina asked, "What did you want to say?"

Roberto gave her a wry look. "I—I want to ask you for your forgiveness, Gina."

His voice shook and Gina thought, forgiveness? Her father was apologizing? She widened her eyes on him. "I don't know what to say, Father."

"How about yes and calling me 'Poppa' again. Father is so formal."

Tears filled her eyes as she looked down at her hands. Her stomach tightened into a hard ball as years of sadness overcame her. Her hand shook as she reached inside her pocket and pulled out a tissue. As she dabbed gently at her eyes, she heard her father heave a deep sigh.

"I didn't want to make you cry—again."

Gina swiveled on the bench to face him. "And I didn't want to cry, but you see, you have this effect on me. Always have. Like I told Stone, it isn't going to be easy to forgive you, especially for forcing me to marry Charlie. Damn it! I was only eighteen."

Brusquely, Roberto said, "If he was so bad for you, why didn't you divorce him then? You were married to him for a long time.

During that time you had little to do with me and the rest of the family and having a second son as well."

For the first time Gina saw what Stone meant about her father and his decision regarding her life. And she had to ask herself why she hadn't divorced Charlie. Because of the boys was certainly one reason, but what about her own personal reasons? The truth was she and Charlie had learned to get along well together. Charlie had been very good to her, even if his high-handedness had irritated the hell out of her.

She could have done worse, and perhaps, as Stone said, her father did what he did at the time because he thought it best for her. And maybe now, in hindsight, it wasn't so bad. After a moment's thought, she also recognized the fact while her marriage to Charlie had been arranged by her father, her love, as it was, had come naturally and had grown over the years for him. But she also knew her feelings for Charlie hadn't been the consuming, blazing love she felt for Stone. But then, she was a woman now and not a little girl. Perhaps that had something to do with it.

"You didn't divorce him because you knew I was right about making you marry him, Gina."

Gina sighed. "At the time I didn't, but now, I suppose I do," she said grudgingly. She glared at him and added, "You know, you've always busted your way into my life, making decisions for me, but you didn't after I married Charlie."

"So, what's your point?"

"Maybe if you had we wouldn't have been estranged all these years," she said softly.

His big brown eyes got bigger as he stared at her. "But I did exactly as you'd wanted me to do for years—I stayed out of your life. I figured you'd come back when you were ready. It broke my heart when you never did. Each time I saw you at a family gathering and you looked right through me, I died a little more inside. It was like losing a child."

Roberto's eyes filled with tears and when he sniffed, Gina

groaned then burst into sobs. Turning to him she threw herself into his arms and he gathered her close. Together they quietly shed tears, holding each other until he set her from him. "We've lost a lot of years together, but no more. Okay?"

She smiled through her tears. "No more." She rose and said, "Come on. We've got to get back and celebrate Christmas."

Gina was surprised when they returned to her house and didn't see Stone's car in the driveway. My Lord, the man had chosen this moment to listen to her for a change. And when she entered the house with her dad, everyone jumped on her case. Her boys, her mother, even her sisters all scolded her. She took it all, quietly, until her father stepped in.

"Why is everybody standing around fighting? Let's get that turkey into the car and get down to Stoney's ranch."

"But, Grandpa," Chris said, "When Stone left, he said he'd be spending another Christmas alone. We wanted him to stay but he wouldn't." Chris glared at his mother. "He said Mom didn't like him much anymore."

Oh, cry me a river, for cryin' out loud! Never had she believed Stone could be so sensitive. Gina said calmly, "We just had a misunderstanding. Now let's get the presents and food packed up." She looked at her father. "Dad, would you call the ranch and let Marguerite—she's Stone's housekeeper—let her know we're on our way. And to tell Stone? The number's on the chalk board on the wall beside the phone."

"Sure thing."

Gina's mother, Ingrid, raised her eyebrows. "You mean you two made up?"

"Absolutely." She gave her mom a quick hug, admiring her stone white hair cut fashionably short. Her mother always had a style of her own and she hadn't changed a bit. Now Gina scolded herself for letting the years go by without seeing much of her parents—because of holding a grudge. Never again, she silently vowed. "Let's get crackin', folks!"

CHAPTER NINETEEN

Her family followed her down to the ranch. Two hours later they opened their trunks and started unloading the Christmas gifts and food.

"Hold it right there!" a voice commanded.

All heads turned toward the house and Stone stood in the doorway looking tall, imposing, and threatening with his lowered brow. "No one takes a damned thing out of those cars until Gina and I have talked." He pierced Gina with a look that made her literally melt in her tracks. He waited, arms folded, as she walked toward him. She held her head high, her eyes daring him to tell her to leave. She smiled to herself knowing he wouldn't do that. He wanted her to stay—forever.

But she was on the defensive, knowing this was the only way she could approach him. She jammed her hands on her hips and tilted her head back to look at him. "No more surprises, Stone. Agreed?"

He twisted his lips and unfolded his arms as he ambled down the steps to meet her. "Okay," he breathed. "Am I forgiven?"

Somewhat grudgingly, she said, "Yes. For your information, I really did plan on making up with dad before telling him about you." She shrugged and gave him a sheepish smile. "Guess I've grown up some since we parted years ago."

He gave her a twisted little smile. "That's great, darlin'."

Gina shivered at the endearment, all the while holding herself back from throwing herself into his arms.

"So," he said. "Are we getting married?"

She heard the trembling in his voice and her heart melted all over again. "Of course we are! You don't think I'd make up with my father for just anyone, do you? All the years of my Mom and sisters harping on me to do it, I never did…until this cowboy comes along and manages to interfere in my life, and"—she reached out and took his hand—"then deftly manages to put things into proper perspective."

He whooped a cowboy holler and swept her into his arms. When he stormed up the stairs with her, she said, "Wait!"

When he did, she looked over his broad shoulder and laughed at the astonished faces. "Come on in, everyone. We're getting married!"

Stone met her brown-eyed gaze and whispered hopefully, his voice low and sensuous, "Today?"

Gina almost said yes when he proceeded to walk slowly with her into the house, not wanting to disappoint him, even as his lips nuzzled at the spot below one earlobe. She pushed him way and said warningly, "Stone…"

"Okay, you're right. We need time to make plans, besides, we'd likely have trouble finding someone to marry us on such short notice."

She grinned. "Yes, *we* do. Thanks for including me."

He threw back his head and laughed as he set her gently on her feet in the kitchen. "You're welcome."

"You know you're going to regret inviting my family for Christmas, don't you?" she said, smiling merrily at him.

He raised his brows and gathered her in his arms again. "Why do you say that?"

She whipped around and nearly laughed aloud at her sons, mom and dad, her sisters, Sofia, and Maria, her husband and six kids standing stone still in the hallway outside the kitchen. They all watched them, expectant expressions on every face. "See those kids? They'll have your ears ringing soon, tinnier than any Christmas bells you've ever heard!"

Stone laughed. "I'll love being with your family, Gina."

She laughed when she noticed his wary gaze focused over her head on all the kids.

He whistled, leaned down, and kissed her cheek. When he moved back his eyes were glistening with tears of happiness. "Luckily, you brought all the food along," he said.

"I've thought of everything, cowboy," she murmured, giving his cheek a quick peck.

———

Stone and Gina had agreed on a spring wedding. That was as long as Stone would wait. Never mind the excuse that the weather would be calmer by then. Who would have ever thought Chicago would get ten inches of snow on her chosen wedding day, May 12th?

Since she'd reunited with her family, she decided to get married back home in Chicago.

The white stuff accumulated before Gina's eyes as she stared out her old bedroom window of her parent's home. Gina had no idea how long she'd been lost in love-struck heaven, which meant thoughts of her husband-to-be, until she heard her bedroom door open and her mother walked in.

Gina glimpsed the time on the clock on her bedside table and gasped. Instead of daydreaming she should have been dressing. "Where is my dress? We're going to be late, Mother!"

"Gina," her mother chided, "you weren't like this when you married Charlie."

"That's because I was young and stupid and didn't know better.

Not wanting to get married probably had something to do with it, too. Besides, you planned my first wedding and it was perfect. I planned this one and I'm afraid I've missed something important."

"Nonsense. You followed that little checklist of things to do over the last few months, didn't you?"

"Yes, and it was a lifesaver."

Gina frowned at the hardwood floor that had been waxed to a high sheen. Everything in her bedroom was the same as it had been fifteen years ago, when she'd left home. "Still, I just have this little feeling..." Pausing, she looked up and smiled into her mother's quizzical expression. She waved her hand carelessly. "It's nothing. I followed that list. I'm confident I haven't missed a single item."

"Excellent," her mother said.

"Ta-da!"

Gina looked toward the doorway and found Maria entering her bedroom, a long plastic bag draped over her arm.

"Wait until you see this dress, Mother. It's to die for!"

Maria carefully laid the gown on the bed, then moved to Gina and hugged her. "I'm so happy for you," she whispered, "You won't believe how delighted Poppa was to get the wedding invitation, not to mention you having the wedding here. He had tears in his eyes."

Guilt permeated Gina, especially when she thought about how she'd denied her sons the chance to get to know their grandfather over the years. The three of them had been inseparable ever since she'd arrived yesterday morning.

An hour later, Gina stood in front of the full-length mirror in her church's dressing room, admiring the beautiful wedding dress.

"That is the loveliest gown I've ever seen," Sofia said as she bustled into the room, dressed in a tea-length rose colored, full-skirted, taffeta gown that looked spectacular on her. Maria followed her sister into the bride dressing room, wearing the same dress as Sofia. She thought her attendants looked beautiful.

"It certainly is," Gina said, taking in the delicate, beaded bodice and the gown's deep vee neckline. The gown's skirt was full, a crinoline beneath to help hold its bell shape. The veil headpiece was a small tiara, and the veil itself long and trailing three feet behind her. She whirled around and hugged Sofia hard.

"I am so happy for you!" Sofia said, her voice choked.

They held hands and smiled at each other then. "Remember when we used to watch Sleeping Beauty, over and over again? And we'd always sing that song, *Someday My Prince Will Come*?"

Gina smiled through her tears. "Someday, Sofia, your prince will come for you. I'm certain of it."

Sofia nodded. "Someday," she said wistfully. Then she grinned. "But I'm having a heck of a good time until then."

Sofia left then and Gina chuckled as she remembered her lovely girlhood moments. She and her sisters had believed they'd fall in love and live happily ever after, like a Princess in fairy tales. Maria had settled for a dependable, older man for her Prince. And now Gina had unexpectedly found the love of her life in this beastly ex-Texas Ranger turned cowboy. She had a strong feeling Sofia's love would enter her life soon.

A knock at the door sounded and a voice bellowed, "Gina, it's time to get married!"

A momentary panic overwhelmed Gina when she heard her father's words. They were the same ones he'd issued to her years ago. Ah, but things were different, and she wasn't, thank the Lord, superstitious.

She checked herself once more in the mirror and opened the door. Her father stood there, dressed in his best suit and tie, beaming down at her, arm cocked and ready to escort her down the aisle. Her sisters were moving up the stairs ahead of her and she knew it was time. Then she heard the organ begin playing Canon in D.

"I'm ready, Poppa." She took a step and scowled when he didn't budge. She looked up into his dear, lined face and whispered, "What's wrong?"

He sighed. "I feel like I've just got my little girl back and I'm losing her again. It doesn't seem fair."

"Oh, Pop! I'll always be your little girl. And I promise we'll visit often."

They took the stairs and she nearly missed a step when he said, "Every weekend."

Gina stumbled and picked up the hem of her gown. "Not possible. San Antonio's over a thousand miles away."

"Once a month, then."

"We'll see. I don't know if Stone can get away from the ranch that often," she said, thankful for the excuse of Falcon's Ridge. She loved her father, but she also knew from the conversation they were currently having he hadn't changed much—if any. Still being his controlling self, but she wouldn't allow it. Not anymore.

"Stoney will find a way to visit often."

"We'll come as often as we can," she said, trying hard not to reveal her exasperation at his insistence.

Her father raised his brow at her. "Some things never change, do they?"

Her frown disappeared and she threw back her head and laughed as he joined her.

They reached the top of the stairs and Gina tugged her father's hand and pulled him along until they reached the long church aisle leading to the altar where her groom stood, proud and tall, and handsome. Maria had walked down the aisle first and now Sofia was midway down it. In about ten seconds it would be Gina's turn.

Gina felt a momentary panic when she saw the faces of friends and family sitting in long pews on either side of the aisle. She smiled when she saw Chris who was standing in the second pew. Her son gave her a big grin and a shy wave. He'd done his role as usher. Connor Wayne, Stone's best man, stood beside him while Jack stood next to Connor. Never would she forget the stunned look on Jack's fifteen-year-old face when Stone had asked him to be a groomsman.

They'd kept the wedding small, having invited only a hundred people, still it was daunting to see so many faces from her past gathered to watch her take this walk in life once more, but with another man. She felt her body tremble a bit and her legs shook as she took small slow steps with her father's robust frame moving side to side. She managed to synchronize her steps to his.

Then Stone's big, strong body at the end of the aisle drew her attention and held it until she reached him. He stood with enviable confidence, tall and straight, legs spread wide, hands folded in front of him. As she drew closer, she saw beneath his gentle smile—saw the nervousness there, knowing it wasn't because he was getting married, but because she'd accepted his proposal and the day had finally arrived.

Her father took her hand and joined it with Stone's. She barely felt her father's peck on the cheek because her eyes were plastered on Stone's loving face. Her smile slipped as she looked her fill of Stone, then she paled.

His smile diminished. He gave the priest a covert look then whispered, "What is it, darlin'?"

"I—I remember what I forgot! Your tuxedo! The one we purchased months ago," she said rather loudly, earning the priest's frown.

Stone glanced down at his black leather jacket, matching leather slacks, white shirt, and black tie. "Let's get married first and talk about it later," he muttered.

And they did.

An hour later they happily exited the church and stood in the pre-planned receiving line with her parents and family to receive their guests and thank them for coming. As Gina accepted a tight hug from her Uncle Vincent, she patted his back and rolled her eyes at a smirking Stone.

By the time the last person passed through the line it was time for them to make their way to the Cascade Inn and Event Center where her parents had insisted on hosting a dinner and dance.

As Stone helped Gina into the limo he'd rented, he murmured, "Now's as good a time as any to let you know you didn't forget the tux. I unpacked it and decided to wear this, instead."

Gina gave an impotent shriek. "What!"

He grinned. "Now don't be mad. I've a pretty strong reason for wearing this suit instead of the tux."

"Give me one good reason, Stone Mitchell, just one!" Gina shouted. Although, deep inside a little voice told her, *Twenty years from now would it really matter?*

He took her resisting body into his arms and kissed her. She immediately quieted when he pinned her against the cushioned seat. Gina was putty in his hands and she relaxed, her eyes misting over with tears of joy. He raised his head after a moment and said, "You ready to hear my reason now without throwing a fit?"

"Yes," she said, hardly able to breath and snatching him back to her when he drew away too far.

"I'll never forget the incredibly sexy look on your face when you saw me in this suit on Christmas. Never." He smiled and pulled her onto his lap, then laughed as he struggled to settle her skirts around them.

She cooperated completely, wound her arms around his neck and kissed him. After a long while she moved back, and he caught the tears falling from her eyes.

With a groan he said, "Oh, geez, tell me you'll forgive me. Please? I'll even pay the photographer to take pictures of us all over again, with me wearing the tux if it means that much to you."

"I don't care about any silly tux. There's nothing to forgive. I love you. You could have met me at the end of the aisle in your 'birthday suit' and it wouldn't change how I feel about you."

Stone growled, "I'll save the birthday suit idea for tonight." He kept her on his lap and rubbed her back until she relaxed against him, finally tucking her head down on his shoulder.

———

It was one o'clock in the morning by the time Gina and Stone arrived at the luxurious hotel room her father had reserved for them for their wedding night.

Gina's feet were killing her. They'd all partied hard, ate and drank too much and danced, but had a memorable, amazing night.

She sat down on the edge of the bed with a groan as she removed the three-inch heeled pumps. When she reached beneath her dress to strip off her stockings Stone was there before her, on his knees and shoving her hands aside.

"Uh-uh. This is my territory," he growled.

Heat seeped into Gina's cheeks at the intimate look in his eyes. She resisted—just a bit—when he pressed his hand against her shoulder until she lay flat on her back on the fluffy white comforter.

As she stared up at the ceiling, her attention was focused on his hot hands on her thigh. He unsnapped one garter from the sexy widow's corset-styled undergarment she'd worn beneath her wedding dress, and then rolled down one stocking. She giggled when he stroked the bottom of her foot, starting to sit up when he murmured, "Not done yet. Got to take off the other one."

She resumed her position as he gave her other leg the same treatment. He finished and her heart started racing when he stroked his hands up and down the insides of her thighs. When he reached the apex of them, he stroked the very center of her until she was a writhing, moaning mess.

He pulled her up to sit on the bed. He sat beside her and managed to ease her out of her gown. She felt awkward with him completely clothed while she was naked. And when she reached out to help him with his jacket he smiled into her eyes.

"I've waited a long time for this day. I want it to last so I've a favor to ask."

"What's that?" she softly said.

"Let's take it real slow."

"If we can."

They took it slow, which made Gina wonder how they'd managed it when they wanted each other. But in the end, with their slippery, heated bodies joined, their movements quickened as they reached for heaven, and climaxed together.

Gina knew with her heart and soul that there had been a master plan all along; they were meant to be together.

EPILOGUE

San Antonio
11 months later

"Push, darlin', push." Stone said, encouraging Gina in her labors to deliver their babies.

"I am!" Gina exclaimed as she sank back on the bed once more as the contractions diminished.

Guilt seeped inside Stone because she was going through this hell to have his children. He hated seeing her in pain and had insisted on being with her through the labor and delivery, even though, at first, he'd been close to fainting when he'd first arrived at the hospital with her.

Stone still couldn't believe it possible that they were having twins—baby girl twins! While siring boys was mighty important to most men, having two little girls that would hopefully take after their mother was satisfying to Stone. Besides, they had Jack and Chris, and Stone felt his family complete with them.

Jack was still stumbling through adolescence but hadn't gotten into any more trouble. At sixteen he'd matured, including surpassing Stone in height. The kid couldn't help but remind him often, coming up and bumping his chest against Stone's, laughing down at him.

He'd taken the boy's prancing peacock attitude in stride, though, but drew the line when Jack had called him 'shorty' one time too often. Stone had eventually put him in his place by taunting him into donning a pair of boxing gloves. They'd sparred at the local gym and Stone showed him who still was boss.

At thirteen, Chris was on the smaller side for his age. Stone figured he took after Gina in looks and disposition and would never likely grow as big as his brother. But Chris attracted the girls like bees to honey with his sweet, fair looks, shy smile, and gentlemanly demeanor. Also, the kid's talent as a musician—playing guitar—helped him gain many a female admirer.

Gina squeezing his hand brought him back to the monumental event happening now. He picked up a cloth and pressed it against her heated forehead. He couldn't recall if he'd ever sweated as much from working the ranch, and knew she was working hard. They'd arrived five hours ago and thankfully, she was making progress, according to the nurses and her doctor.

She groaned and formed her hands against her swelled abdomen and gritted out, "Here comes another one."

He sat beside her on the hospital bed, rubbed her stomach in circles, amazed by the strength of the movement and tightening beneath his hands. Never had he ever felt anything so powerful.

"Oh, oh," she groaned louder, warning him that something was happening out of the ordinary.

"The babies are coming!" she said, gasping and, raising her knees, she planted her feet on the bed as she huffed and puffed.

"You sure?" Stone asked, rising to his feet.

Her eyes narrowed on him as, between heavy breathing, she said in a sarcastic tone, "No, I've never done this before."

"Sorry," he mumbled, "of course you'd know."

"Buzz for the doctor," she said wearily, after the contraction subsided. "I...I need to push!"

Soon the room was bustling with two nurses and two doctors to accommodate a twin birth. Within an amazingly short amount of time, at least in Stone's mind, his daughters made their way into the world. Birthing was an amazing thing! After his second daughter was born, Stone felt lightheaded, grasped the back of the nearest chair but fell. As he hit the floor, pain exploded in his head. Then nothing.

———

Gina sat propped up in the newly made up bed and breathed a sigh of relief that her laboring had ended. They'd ended up with two healthy daughters, even if they were a bit small and would need to spend a few weeks growing in the hospital before they could take them home. She had just brought baby Angela to her breast when baby Marissa started screeching at the top of her lungs where she lay in her tiny bed beside Angela's bed.

She frowned, tried to decide how to continue feeding one baby while reaching for the other when she heard bedclothes rustling from the other bed. She looked over at Stone who'd pulled back the covers and stumbled to his feet.

"I'll hold her off 'til you're done," he offered.

Gina grinned as she watched Stone trudge across the floor.

"You sure? I mean, are you feeling better now?"

He gave her a chagrinned look. "I'm never going to live this down, you know. I mean how many guys faint while their wives are in labor, after all?"

She laughed. "Lots, from what Doctor Anderson told me. The good thing was you didn't pass out until after the twins were born. You were a trooper 'til the very end. I'm proud of you."

"Don't say a word about this to Jack," he said as he picked up his squalling daughter. "I'll never hear the end of it."

"Uh, oh. He already knows. You were passed out in the bed when they tip-toed in to see the babies. Sorry, I had to tell them why you were dead-out, not to mention the fact I had to explain how you got the big purple bruise."

Stone grimaced and gingerly touched the goose egg on his forehead. "Damn, I thought I'd gotten a better grip on that chair."

He scowled at the chair then sat beside her, placing his stocking-clad feet on the lower bedrail as he propped his daughter on his knees. Gina smiled as he talked baby chatter to her, unable to believe this big, strong guy was such a softy.

His eyes met hers then and he whispered, "You've made me very happy, sweetheart. You and the kids mean everything to me, and always will."

Tears welled in her own eyes as she nodded and bit her lips. "Ditto," she said, her voice wobbling.

She sank back and closed her eyes as she enjoyed the gentle suckling of the baby; enjoyed this intimate moment with her husband and children, knowing there was nothing sweeter in her life.

Gina didn't care one bit that Stone wasn't much like a prince from one of her girlhood fairy tales, for in her mind this gentle cowboy would always be her king, husband, friend, and lover.

No, she'd never regret marrying her cowboy, with only a few rugged edges.

THE END

———

THANK YOU FOR READING

Did you enjoy this book?

We invite you to leave a review at your favorite book site, such as Goodreads, Amazon, Barnes & Noble, etc.

DID YOU KNOW THAT LEAVING A REVIEW...

- Helps other readers find books they may enjoy.
- Gives you a chance to let your voice be heard.
- Gives authors recognition for their hard work.
- Doesn't have to be long. A sentence or two about why you liked the book will do.

ABOUT THE AUTHOR

Nancy Schumacher is the owner-publisher of Melange Books, LLC, writing under the pseudonyms, Nancy Pirri and Natasha Perry.

She is a member of Romance Writers of America. She is also one of the founders of the RWA chapter, Northern Lights Writers (NLW), in Minnesota.

www.nancypirri.com

 facebook.com/NancyPirriAuthor

ALSO BY NANCY PIRRI

Montana Women

Katie and the Marshal

Annie and the Outlaw

Janie and the Judge

Laura and the Railroad Baron

The Montana Women Boxset

Contemporary Romance

Bait Shop Blue

All I Ever Wanted

I Wish You Love, a Spicy Romance Anthology

Make Me Behave (An Anthology) with Tara Fox Hall

Historical Romance

The MacAulay Bride

The Duke and the Lady Sleuth

A Husband For Christmas

Featured in the following anthologies:

Western Ways

Food and Romance Go Together, Vol. 2

Writing erotica as Natasha Perry

Ruined Hearts

Maid of His Heart